About the author

During the 1960s and 1970s, Ray spent much time skiing in the Swiss resorts, both the fashionable ones and the lesser known ones in the more remote parts of the Alps. His knowledge of these areas enables him to bring the true atmosphere and reality of the locations, which adds to the enjoyment of the story.

During the 1980s, Ray had five books published in his *Horsekeeping* series, drawing on his many years of experience with horses.

His autobiography, *How Lucky Can You Get*, is available and he is now working on a sequel to this novel.

HIGH SPY

Ray Saunders

HIGH SPY

Vanguard Press

VANGUARD PAPERBACK

A CIP catalogue record for this title is
available from the British Library.

ISBN 978 1 784658 51 9

*Vanguard Press is an imprint of
Pegasus Elliot MacKenzie Publishers Ltd.*
www.pegasuspublishers.com

First Published in 2020

**Vanguard Press
Sheraton House Castle Park
Cambridge England**

Printed & Bound in Great Britain

Dedication

My thanks to my nephew, Grant Moody, and to Richard Lavender, for their help with technical input to the book, and to my production coordinator, Vicky Gorry, for her contribution.

Chapter 1

I sat down at the table and waited for the familiar steps of my housekeeper bringing breakfast.

It wasn't long before she entered the room and came towards me.

"Morning, ducks," she said, setting the tray down on the table.

"Morning, Flo," I replied.

"You're looking bleedin' miserable this mornin'," she said. "You look like old Sam Rye down the bettin' shop when he pays me out for a twenty to one winner."

I grinned up at her. Flo had been with me almost ten years and wouldn't admit her age, but I knew that she drew her pension. A widow for many years, she had a zest for life, and I'd never seen anything that could get her down.

"Thought you was going on 'oliday this month, 'ave you made arrangements yet?" she asked.

"Well as far as the business goes, I can leave at any time," I said. "Robert can cope quite easily without me at this time of year." Robert was the manager of my estate agency business that I'd set up from the money a spinster aunt had left me.

"Well then, why don't you nip orf and 'ave a bit of

fun." She was hustling around me with the breakfast. "Find y'self a bit of skirt, I expect that's your trouble, why you've been so bleedin' moody lately."

I laughed. "You could be right, Flo," I said. "It's time I had a break, but I've been waiting for the snow reports to improve, there's not a lot of snow out there at the moment."

Flo sat down opposite me and poured the tea. "I thought it was always snow in Switzerland in the winter, because of the mountains," she said.

"Not always enough for good skiing, Flo. It only comes at certain times and it's late this year."

"Then why don't you go somewhere warm where you can lie on the beach all day?" She persisted.

"Because I like to ski, there's no other sensation quite like it," I replied.

"You wouldn't catch me slithering down no bleedin' mountain in the middle of winter, it must be cold enough to freeze the tits off a Chinese porcupine." She paused then went on. "Anyway, why go all that way for a bit of crumpet, there's plenty nearer home."

I swallowed some toast. "That, Flo, is only secondary," I joked with her. "The skiing is of first importance, besides when conditions are good the sun can be pretty strong, and you don't feel the cold."

"Why don't it melt the snow then?" she asked.

"Because of the altitude," I said.

"Oh."

I finished breakfast and she began clearing away.

"I'll probably be pushing off in a day or so," I said. "The forecast is for heavy snow in the Alps."

Flo reached the door, and pushing it open with the tray, she paused as she went through. "When you collect the papers, don't forget to tell them to keep my Sportin' Life," she said. "Old Sam Rye's stopped 'aving it down the bettin' shop, and I can't make 'ead nor tail of those bleedin' wall sheets."

"Okay," I called after her, smiling to myself. Flo wouldn't care if a tidal wave or earthquake struck, she'd still insist on having her daily Guinness and her bet. It was this indomitable spirit that had served to bring her and millions like her through the Blitz.

It was sleeting as I left home, and arriving at the car park, I ran the short distance to the office. I spent the morning signing cheques to cover the bills and wages while I was away. I told Robert I wouldn't be in for a month and that I'd phone him with my whereabouts. He was quite happy to take over, and after we'd discussed a few details, I left. Driving home, my thoughts turned to my holiday. Flo had been right. I needed to get off for some fun, and a 'bit of skirt', as she put it, wouldn't go amiss for après-ski either.

The following morning, I fitted the ski rack to the car roof, loaded my equipment and prepared to leave. After breakfast, Flo saw me off as I left for Dover.

"Don't forget to send me a card!" she called as I waved goodbye.

By early afternoon I had crossed the Channel and

was driving through northern France. I had made this trip many times, but it never failed to give me a feeling of elation once I was heading for Switzerland. The prospect of snow and sun with that special atmosphere both climatic and social, that you only get from mountain skiing, always excited me.

Passing through Rheims, I continued on to Chaumont, for my usual overnight stop at the Grand Val Hotel, run by two sisters. Madame always greeted me, and the head waiter, whom I had nicknamed Trigger, always remembered me by the tip I gave him. Salmon Parisienne for starters, followed by coq au vin and a bottle of madame's red wine, was always my dinner, followed by a good night's' sleep.

The next morning was overcast. Passing through Pontarlier, the snow that had threatened all day began falling heavily, as I crossed the Jura. As the sky darkened, the blinding snowflakes raced towards the car like white tracer bullets. It soon built up each side of the windscreen as the wipers struggled to cope. I stopped and fitted the chains and continued to the border. Once I dropped down towards Lake Geneva the snow had stopped, and removing the chains, I continued up the Rhone valley to Brig. The Zermatt train was waiting, and after parking my car, I loaded my skis and baggage and settled in a seat by the window.

Looking out at the passing scene, my mind thought back on my life. I'd been evacuated during the war and my parents had been killed during the Blitz. An old aunt had brought me up, until I entered the army at eighteen and joined the Army Physical Training Corps. After a thirty-week course, I served out my time as a sergeant physical training instructor (PTI), attached to various regiments. My aunt had died soon after I left the army, and the money she had left me had enabled me to start my business. It left me with no other family, and although I'd had several relationships, none had resulted in my wanting to settle down with them. Maybe I was destined to become a confirmed old bachelor.

The train reached Zermatt and I soon found my hotel and checked in.

For nine wonderful days, I enjoyed skiing in perfect snow conditions, then for no particular reason save for a nostalgic desire to visit some old acquaintances, I decided to spend the rest of my holiday in the small village of Riederalp further up the valley. It was one of those decisions seeming at the time of no great importance but stemming from which the future pattern of your life would change.

I breakfasted leisurely on the simple but delicious 'fruhstuck' provided by the Hotel Garni Alpina: my favourite bread rolls, cricket ball shaped and crusty, spread with butter and eaten with several assorted Swiss cheeses, which were always placed next to them on the crisp, white tablecloth and fresh, hot coffee, drunk from a breakfast cup that had been thoughtfully arranged with a paper drip mat to separate it from the saucer. I finished the remaining rolls and butter with a selection of individual 'confitures', from which I always selected the black cherry.

Returning to my room, I stepped out onto the balcony into the morning sun. Leaning on the rails, I looked down at the scene spread out before me like a glorious technicolour movie. A boulder-strewn river tumbled along down the valley, and the sound of its progress as it raced over the large ice platforms came drifting up like music. A naked deciduous tree clung to the steep snowbank overhanging the water, its bare branches, white with frost, releasing faint clouds of mist that drifted up to evaporate in the warm rays of the sun. The rooftops below were already dripping away their heavy blankets of snow, as the sun's rays crept steadily across them. Many of the hotels had their windows shuttered, as they waited for the season to begin in earnest.

I adjusted my sunglasses and looked across at the church that was tucked neatly into the centre of this old alpine village. The clock beneath its fine old spire chimed the hour, as I drew in a deep breath, filling my lungs with the still mountain air, and feeling the heady lift from its pureness. Looking up, I viewed the mighty Matterhorn towering above the village, the magnificence of its crooked peak standing like a giant sentinel against the deep blue sky. This was Zermatt.

Returning to my room, I packed my things into my large, old valise that swallowed everything, and zipping it up, I noticed the worn leather corners that betrayed the fact that it had travelled with me for many years. Carrying it through the door, I took the lift down and left it beside the reception desk while I went for my skis. On returning, I settled the bill, shouldered my skis, grabbed my bag and made off for the station. A workman was clearing the overnight snow from the skating rink, and the smell of his cheroot was clearly discernible from fifty yards away as it polluted the clean morning air. In front of the station were several horse-drawn buses that the larger hotels used to fetch their guests as they arrived. The horses relentlessly pawed the frozen ground and tossed their heads impatiently, causing the harness bells to jingle noisily, as the clouds of vapour came from their gaping nostrils.

How long would it be, I wondered, before the road that only came partly up the valley, was extended to bring cars and fumes to spoil the atmosphere and charm of this old-style village.

It was such a grand morning I couldn't resist the opportunity to enjoy another experience of the overnight fall of powder snow. I had plenty of time to get to Riederalp and the conditions on the north-facing slopes of the glacier high above would be perfect.

Leaving my valise with the luggage room attendant, I first unzipped it and tucked my passport and travel documents inside and also my car keys, as I wouldn't need them on the mountain. I tipped the attendant and told him that I would pick it up later. The Gornergrat Bahn was opposite, and being low season there were only a few skiers standing about waiting for the next train.

I checked my watch by the large electric clock above the entrance, and reading the timetable, found there were only ten minutes to wait for the next train. It arrived on time, and after leaving my skis in the end alcove, I found a seat by the window on the sunny side. Minutes later the postal, telegraph and telephone (P.T.T.) carriage was clonking and straining its way up to Riffelalp and on through the snow tunnels to Riffelberg. It continued to slowly wind its way up to Gornergrat, where it arrived some fifty minutes later.

The view across the Gornergletcher was breath-taking. It was dominated by the massive domed top of the Monte Rosa, standing over fourteen thousand feet high as it guarded the Italian border, with the lesser peaks of the range that stretched away towards the Theodul Pass and the Matterhorn.

It was markedly colder at this altitude, despite the midday sun, and I zipped up my anorak as I made my way across to the two-stage cable car that takes good skiers up past Hohtalligrat to ten thousand feet on the Stockhorn. Only half a dozen others shared the cable cabin with me. By their conversation they were Italians, and when we reached the top, they made off on the lower route down towards Triftji.

Fixing my skis, I chose the north-facing route and was soon skirting the crevasse below Stockhorn and enjoying the deserted fresh snow of the two-mile run above the Rote Nase glacier. Crossing the ridge, I let the skis gather speed, and with a series of wide turns, I made the final descent back to Gornergrat. The snow was perfect, of the kind that is difficult to find with crowded runs and mechanically maintained pistes. An opportunity like this had to be exploited to the full.

Reaching the bottom, I went up again and took the same route back. This time, using my previous tracks as a guide, I sped downhill enjoying the exhilaration, as I carved out patterns in the powder snow fields.

Back at the bottom I skied across to the restaurant and after thrusting my skis into the snowbank outside, I clonked my way up the icy steps to the long self-service counter. Eggs, bacon and an enormous portion of chips, salty and very hot, together with a jug of red wine went down well and would sustain me until my evening meal in Riederalp.

With the warmth from the meal and wine spreading through me, I decided to go up once more. This time I would ski down to Triftji and take the tow back to Rote Nase. Then I'd make the descent to Findela and take the train back to Zermatt. Then down to Brig to collect my car and drive along to Morel in time to take the telepherique up to Riederalp before it closed.

This would make an excellent finish to the day. A steep descent for almost four miles, the last part finishing through trees just above the station. Only skied when conditions were favourable, it needed split second timing and a high degree of skill. With the thought of this, my adrenalin rose.

As I left the restaurant, the sun had lost its strength. I headed for the cable car. Standing alone in the cabin as it swung out from Hohtalligrat, I noticed far below that the Triftji lift that I would need to take me back to the Rote Nase wasn't running. This meant making a diversion across the top of Stockhorn then down the Findela glacier to Triftji and the Findela station. I would have to trudge upwards towards Stockhorn before I could traverse the glacier, and the snow across the ridge would be very deep. I had only made this descent once before, accompanied by a guide, but felt sure I could remember the way down.

Leaving the cable car, the wind blowing the loose snow off the ridge, I began to climb towards the summit. Despite the marked drop in temperature, perspiration trickled down my forehead from the effort of the climb. It was too late to turn back, so I resolutely plodded on. Twenty minutes later I was high enough for the diversion across the glacier, so I pushed off downhill and quickly gathered speed.

Making a series of jump turns to avoid the rocky outcrops, I became intoxicated by the joy of free movement through the wide expanse of virgin snow. It blinded my caution as I floated down, and it wasn't until my momentum slackened that I realised I had gone much too far. I was now very much lower, and on the wrong side, to be able to link up in the way I'd planned. Telling myself I'd be lucky to get to Riederalp that night,

I began the long climb back up the slope. It was soon obvious that I would never make it. Running downhill through the deep snow had been easy but endeavouring to climb back up was impossible. The snow was so soft and deep I had difficulty in lifting each ski for the upward side-step. What's more, the steepness of the snowfield rising above me presented a danger of an avalanche. Disturbing this lower base could precipitate a snow slide that would engulf me in seconds.

I stood for a minute contemplating what to do. My best bet was to traverse around the snowfield to my right and hope that it would lead to another lift. I could then use it to take me back to the other side. There were several routes down to Italy with connecting lifts, but it was doubtful if they would be running this early in the season. I was on the wrong side of the Monte Rosa for the Cervinia complex, and as far as I could judge the direction from memory, my nearest ski run would be several miles to the east at Macugnaga below the Monte Moro Pass.

My next worry was the lengthening shadows that were spreading across the white desert as the sun lost height and dropped away below the peaks. Late afternoon was no time to be stranded at ten thousand feet in the Alps. Even in daylight, temperatures dropped well below freezing, and only God knew what it plummeted to here after dark. As the shadows deepened there was nothing before me except an everlasting expanse of blank snow. High above the tree line at this altitude there is no form of shelter, and I'd be a goner if I couldn't find a way down to lower ground before nightfall.

I cursed myself for my predicament. Guide- books always emphasize that visitors to Zermatt should never ski off-piste alone, at these high altitudes. Only last year three local guides had been swept to their deaths while attempting to place 'lawinen' markers to warn of the danger of avalanches. I cursed my stupidity at being lost amid the highest and loneliest mountains in Europe, with nightfall approaching. If I didn't make it, the night spots would be humming with stories of the mysterious disappearance of an Englishman.

All of my previous exuberance now gone, I skied on cautiously, with frequent stops to pick my way through snowbanks and steep gullies. As I rounded the side of a peak, I emerged at last into sunlight once more. Stretching away below me was a skiable slope towards the tree line and what looked to be the Italian ski stations. I scanned the slopes for any sign of activity but there was none. Then, just above the first line of trees I saw a half-buried hut. It was the unmistakable shape of a mountain hut and its presence meant I could spend a cold, but safe night there, and continue the next morning.

With the relief at escaping a freezing death from exposure on the glacier, my bladder reminded me that the half litre of plonk that I'd drunk was now surplus to requirements. Facing the low sun, I planted my sticks firmly in the snow, and removing one glove, I unzipped the front of my ski pants. I fished inside for Percy, but he didn't much fancy being pulled out to face the coldness and shrank back into the hairy warmth of my testicles, which had snuggled themselves tight into my crutch. Dragging him free, I pointed him at the ground and joyfully released a gush of hot piss, which sent up a cloud of steam as I wrote my name with orange channels through the snow.

"He who pees and skis away, lives to ski another day," I joked out loud to myself.

Tucking Percy away, I zipped up, put on my glove and, grabbing my ski sticks, jumped off in the direction of the hut. I then saw some fresh tracks, and encouraged by their presence, I followed them down.

I wasn't alone. Sticking in the snow outside the door were two skis and a pair of ski sticks that had fallen over beside them. This meant company for the night and it was probably a forest worker who could guide me down.

Releasing my skis, I pushed open the door and went inside. The dim interior was made worse by my sunglasses, and pushing them up onto my forehead, I looked around for my companion. There was no one there, and puzzled by the omission, I was about to go back outside when a distant chugging sound caused me to pause and listen. It quickly increased to the unmistakable sound of an approaching helicopter. I hurried outside to scan the sky as the noise drew nearer. As I spotted the chopper coming in low over the trees, I also sensed a movement in the snow behind me. Half turning, I was just in time to flinch forwards as something heavy struck me across the back of my head and shoulders. The glimpse of a man holding a rifle above me was my last recollection, as I pitched forwards into oblivion.

Chapter 2

Consciousness began to return like a tide ebbing and flowing across the sands, as awareness gradually filtered through my brain. I opened my eyes and blinked several times, but it made no difference to the darkness that surrounded me. Moving my legs or attempting to sit up caused a dagger-sharp pain to shoot through me. Lowering myself down again, I remained still for several minutes, waiting for it to ease off. It slowly subsided and I was ready to try again. Cautiously easing myself up onto one elbow, I was then able to stand up. I felt cold and stiff, but the pain was bearable this time.

Everywhere was darkness except for the tiny white star-like sparks that floated in front of my eyes. I groped about with one hand and felt the wooden bunk that I'd been lying on. As my head cleared, I saw a small chink of light coming from beneath a door. Fully conscious now, I made towards it but with my second step I stumbled over some poles that scraped loudly on the wooden floor. Pitching forwards, I instinctively reached out to save myself, and caught hold of something that gave way and crashed down, taking me with it. Then came the sound of running feet and voices coming towards me. There was a rattling of bolts and the door burst open. From the illumination, I was able to catch a quick glimpse of a light, shining from another room at the end of a long, wooden passage.

I was in what looked to be a storeroom with a bunk, an old wooden table and a shelf with lamps on it, but that was all I was able to take in. This was enough to tell me something; it was typical of the dark, old wooden chalets found in the remote mountain areas of Switzerland close to the Italian border.

Lying there, I attempted to untangle myself from the wooden poles strewn around me, but then my attention was taken by the man who stood outlined in the doorway. He advanced into the room, carrying an old-fashioned lamp that he placed heavily on the table. Two other men came in and, pulling me to my feet, they dragged me back to the bunk, throwing me heavily onto it. The three of them seemed to be arguing with each other in a dialect I couldn't interpret. Obviously, the leader, the first one came over and leaned down towards me until his face was close to mine. He was a big, wide-shouldered man, and looking up at his face I could see his heavy features. His nose was long and crooked, and his thick wide lips curled back over large, almost square teeth as he spoke. Again, it was the dialect that I couldn't understand, and I was left to just stupidly look up to him. Angered by my silence, his voice became louder and more excited until he was screaming at me.

Turning my head to avoid his garlic-laden breath, I felt bewildered and vulnerable. Reaching down, he grabbed my head and wrenched it around to face him, continuing to shout at me as he did.

Utterly confused, I could only think of stammering, "Non comprends," and this only angered him more. Reaching below his jacket, he came out with a heavy revolver. Clutching it in his thick, hairy fingers, he prodded the barrel against my chest, continuing the ranting that reverberated around my head. Clearing my throat, I said, "I'm English, what do you want? Do you speak English?" It seemed to calm him down and he turned and spoke to the other men. Thinking that I'd managed to get through to him, I began getting up from the bunk. The next moment the other two grabbed me and pinned back my arms as Garlic Mouth turned to me once more. Without warning, he struck me viciously across the face with the back of his hand, knocking my head sideways. The blow stung badly and before it had died down, he repeated it in the other direction.

I'd never in my life taken a beating without giving a good account of myself no matter what the odds. Bullies never chose me twice and I was incensed at being made a whipping boy. With only my legs free to move, I lashed out with my feet and connected somewhere in the region of Garlic Mouth's groin, pushing him back away from me. Failing to free my arms, I could only roll my head and shoulders as he came at me again. Then there was a girl's voice as another light appeared in the doorway. Garlic Mouth backed away from me and I could see the girl standing there. She had a roundish figure, was rather short in stature and wore dark ski pants and a thick, roll-necked jumper that made her bust look abnormally large for her height.

Putting the lamp, she was carrying on the table, she placed a metal bowl beside it from which she took a hypodermic syringe. As the others held me down, she approached and stood over me, adjusting the needle. Garlic Mouth spoke to her and I didn't need an interpreter to know what was about to happen. From my previous semi-consciousness, I remembered this happening before.

Fury swept over me, and I wrenched my arms free and leapt off the bunk, knocking the girl backwards. Grabbing the bowl as the only weapon available to me, I lashed out in an arc, hitting one man in the face, knocking him backwards. With the way clear, I made for the door and once through, I was sure that I could outrun a gazelle with my adrenalin surging.

I never made it.

Garlic Mouth swung round, hitting me in the face with his revolver. The impact of the blow caused me to drop the bowl, and I staggered backwards, feeling the warm blood trickling down my cheek.

"You bastard!" I spat out and grabbing a pole from the floor I started towards him.

"I'll break your fucking neck," I hissed at him through clenched teeth and would have but for being grabbed by the other man.

The pole was long and clumsy at close range, and as I struggled, Garlic Mouth renewed his attack on me. "I kill you!" he screamed, and raising the revolver, he struck me with a blow I was helpless to avoid.

I felt the floor move away from under me, and vaguely felt my sleeve being pulled up, then everything was darkness again.

I came round sprawled on the rough wooden floor. I lay there collecting my thoughts, trying to piece together what had happened and forcing my brain to function logically.

Focusing my attention on how to get away, I saw the dim light from beneath the door, and as I listened, I could hear voices from along the corridor. Cautiously getting to my feet, I tried desperately to recall the details of the layout. I gradually moved around the walls, feeling in the darkness for anything that could be knocked down as I had no wish to trigger a repetition of the last episode. The walls were solid, and the heavy door was obviously bolted on the outside.

Leaning back against the rough wall a wave of panic swept over me, the like of which I'd never known before. What the hell was I doing here?

Summoning up my self-control, I forced the panic down until calm returned to me.

"I must get away from this place," I whispered to myself. "I must — I must." But how?

I slid down the wall to squat on the floor by the door. The floor!

That was it. There had been a draught of cold air through the uneven boards when I'd been lying on them. If this was an old Walliser chalet it would be built on stilts to compensate for the winter snow. And beneath the floor would be a space that led to freedom.

Kneeling forwards, I began tracing the joins of the floor with my fingers. The planks were rough and irregular, with gaps where shafts of air wafted through. If I could prize one up there would be a way to escape. I began pulling at the planks with my fingers, but nothing would budge.

"It's no use, I'll have to find something to lever them up with," I muttered. "What was on that shelf?"

I stood up and gently felt along the shelf until my fingers came to what I could feel was a lamp.

Lifting it gently, I held my breath as I slowly lowered it. Nothing else came crashing down and as all about me remained silent, I started breathing again. Feeling around the lamp there was a thick wire handle making a loop at the top. These handles usually hooked into the sides and, feeling for the point of insertion, I held it against my anorak to deaden the sound, then pulled and twisted the wire until it came out. I could now make a hook and push it through the floorboards to pull one up.

"Beautiful," I said joyously.

Twisting it so that it hooked beneath the board, I began pulling it in an effort to move the plank.

As I pulled with all the strength I could muster, the

wire suddenly straightened, resulting in me yanking it out of the crack.

"Shit!" I exploded, throwing it into the black void that surrounded me. Immediately frightened that my outburst had been heard, I crouched, listening for the sound of boots coming along the corridor. Several seconds passed and nothing happened. They had probably kipped down for the night. Taking up the lamp again, I fingered its outline and found the flat circular top that unscrewed as I twisted it. It was thin enough to insert into the cracks and was made of stout metal.

Satisfied, I quickly pushed it into a crack and used it as a lever. My hand couldn't exert enough force, so I stood up and used the heel of my boot. Though I bore down on it with a continuous pressure, the plank still wouldn't budge. I was about to try another plank when it occurred to me what was wrong.

"You're standing on the bloody plank," I said, rebuking myself, and shifting sideways I repeated the heel pressure. There was then the unmistakeable movement of the floorboard lifting.

"Thank Christ."

Slowly at first, and then with a jerk, my ski boot flattened the lid and the board popped up. Quickly reaching down, I curled my fingers under it, and pulling with a new-found strength, it came up easily as the nails released it.

Beneath me now was a narrow rectangle of greyness about a metre in length. Using the plank that

I'd freed as a lever, I soon had the next board dislodged.

I quickly lay down beside the opening and taking a pole, I lowered it through until it bottomed out.

"Smashing." Gripping it, I lowered myself through and was about halfway down when there was a sudden tug on my anorak that had caught on a nail. Trying to pull myself back up, I wrapped my legs around the pole and drew myself up to release it. Suddenly an agonising cramp caught me behind the thigh, forcing me to quickly straighten my leg for relief, and the next moment I shot down the pole to the accompaniment of a loud ripping noise.

"Sod it!"

Hoping the soft earth had muffled the noise, I paused for a moment to listen. Nothing happened so I crept forwards towards the light from behind a pile of logs. The moon appeared from behind a cloud, flooding the landscape with its silvery beam, reflecting on the snow that was intersected with vast, dark areas of pine forest. Baring my left wrist, I could see the face of my old Belvil watch illuminated by the moonlight. Holding it closer, I squinted to bring the dial into focus. It was just after midnight.

A large sledge was lying upside down, its ski-shaped runners uppermost. I ran to it and squatted down to survey my surroundings. It was much colder here, and a shiver ran through me as the rawness of the night air bit into me. The outer layer of my anorak was ripped at the shoulder but was otherwise intact. I pulled up the collar and wished that I'd searched for my gloves and hat before I'd left.

Little dark clouds occasionally flitted across the enormous moon, momentarily dimming its light, as thousands of stars twinkled in the otherwise clear sky. Even in my present predicament I marvelled at the incredible beauty that spread out before me.

Further in front of me there was a large level rectangle of flattened snow that appeared to end abruptly at its further perimeter. With a quick look back to see that the chalet was still in darkness, I made my way across the snow and then saw a large barn-like building on the other side. Hurrying on, I circled it and came around to the front which had large double doors. There were numerous ski tracks like tram lines leading away from it, and further on I could see that they ended abruptly where there was a ravine that dropped away and was bounded by trees on its far side. Then I noticed a tall pole hanging motionless, from which was the unmistakable shape of a wind pocket.

"This must be a helicopter pad!" I exclaimed. "And this barn must be the hangar."

As I stood in the semi darkness, the moon came out again, giving me chance to examine the doors. They were hung on metal runners suspended on rollers that allowed them to slide past each other. Gripping one edge, I pulled hard and it began to open. Going inside, I paused to adjust to the gloominess, then saw that there wasn't a chopper inside, just a large snow-clearing machine. Looking beyond it to the far wall, I saw shadowy objects that I couldn't make out until I moved closer.

"Well I'm buggered, hang-gliders!"

The reason that the ski trails ended abruptly in front of the barn was now obvious. It was where they launched off into the air.

During my army service I'd spent three months with the Parachute Regiment and made a few practice jumps. My commanding officer had been keen on hang-gliding and he'd once taken me up as a tandem passenger. I knew the basics but had never tried it solo.

While I was pondering what to do, I looked through the doors to the chalet. Two yellow rectangles of light appeared, outlining the windows.

Next to the hang-gliders were several pairs of skis. Grabbing a pair, I took a delta wing and carried them both outside. The skis' bindings were too large for my boots, and, swearing, I ran back for another pair. This time I was successful, and I thrust my boots into the open bindings, pushed my hands through the loops in the ski sticks and picked up the delta wing. Quickly buckling the harness, I pushed off, following the ski trails.

Shouting came from the chalet and meant that Garlic Mouth and his trio had discovered my absence and would soon be looking for me.

My progress was slow, and I had difficulty propelling myself whilst holding the delta wing. Next a buzzing noise flashed past, followed immediately by the sharp crack of a shot. Two more shots rang out, the sound much closer now.

Spurring on my legs to greater effort, I began sliding along on the sloping snow towards the ravine. "Faster — for God's sake faster," I prayed aloud, fearing that my pursuers were gaining on me.

Then came speed, lovely speed, uncontrolled and alarming, and the wind whistled past my ears as I raced along down the steepening slope. Then I felt a strange lightness and realised with mounting terror that my skis were no longer in contact with the ground.

I zoomed on and upwards as more shouts came from below, with another shot that now seemed a long way behind me.

"So far, so good," I said, not daring to look down. In the heat of the moment there hadn't been time to worry about the consequences, so long as I got away. Now, hanging below this sail, the full implications of what I'd done were only too clear. Making myself look down, I could make out the darkened valley, with trees and large blotches of snow below me. Surely, I was gaining height!

My next sensation as my nerves settled, was to feel how cold I was as it bit into my hands. My face and ears were stinging, and my hands were going numb. Then I realised I wasn't gaining height; it was the valley sloping away beneath me that caused this impression. Looking ahead, I was in fact below the skyline and heading towards a mountain on the other side. Pulling with one arm, I shot sideways and began dropping at an alarming rate. The ground came racing up towards me and not knowing what to do, I did something, and my heart stopped as I thought I'd stalled. Then I levelled out and drifted down at a more sedate speed and less fearful angle. Next, I was sailing along above the trees and spotting a large area of snow ahead of me.

"That's got to be it," I muttered. "Hold on — here we go."

I drew up my legs to clear the last of the trees and the skis felt like pendulous weights to my numbed limbs, causing me to crab side to side as I descended. Angling the tips upwards, I prepared for the landing as the snow raced up to meet me.

The moment of touchdown wasn't as bad as I had feared and surprised me with its gentleness. "Perfect, bloody perfect, you, clever old bugger," I shouted joyously to myself, and instantly regretted the remark as I accelerated along the snow field.

Attempting to snow plough to a stop, I crossed my skis, and pitched forwards with legs, skis and glider all tangled together on top of me. I was half-buried in the snow, looking up at the starry heaven from whence I had just descended.

"Matt, you've made it!" I exclaimed.

I fumbled about trying to free myself, but I could hardly feel my fingers and all their strength had gone. Trying to regain circulation, I beat both hands against my chest, shook them violently and then poked each one in turn into my mouth for warmth. A little better from this, I blew on them, feeling my breath rattle the icicles that hung from my moustache. Struggling up, I knocked off the loose snow and my thoughts turned to Garlic Mouth and the others who would by now probably be pursuing me. They might have another way down and any second another bullet from a high velocity rifle could be hurtling towards me.

Adjusting my skis, I pushed off, not knowing if I was in Switzerland or over the border in Italy.

I silently resolved not to take any chances as I pressed on down the valley. Then in front of me I saw a light. It was just a twinkle some way off and below me about a mile away. The snow wasn't as deep here, and neither were there any steep places to negotiate in the moonlight. I then found obstacles like old fencing posts and wire that made progress slow and difficult. The moon, which had served me so well, was now hiding its face occasionally, behind patches of black cloud that were creeping across the sky from the mountains. I lost sight of the light several times but urged myself on till at last I was close enough to make out where the light was coming from. Several buildings were huddled together at the end of a narrow ribbon of road that widened to form a small square.

I pushed on until I came to the largest building that had an enormous roof that overhung the stone steps leading up to the door. There were several lights around the square and taking off my skis I crept over to the corner of the building. I couldn't tell how far I'd come and knew that parts of the Italian Alps close to the border were inhabited by bandits. Even during the war, the Germans never entered these parts. As I stood sizing up the situation, the first small snowflakes began unhurriedly drifting down through the yellowy illumination.

This could be where the Garlic Mouth gang operated from. I stealthily crept to the corner and there, not twenty feet away was a small truck. It was facing away from me, but I could smell the cigarette smoke of the person who was crouched over the steering wheel. It could be that Garlic Mouth had radioed down to him to watch out for me. Why else would anyone be waiting there at this time? I had no weapon and would have no chance against him, as he would obviously be armed.

Looking around, I saw a wood pile and selected a piece about two feet long that made a weighty cudgel. As I crept towards the back of the truck, I could see that the cab was the open type without a door, similar to the types that I'd driven in the army. Moving along the driver's side, I raised the cudgel and kicked the side of the chassis. It had the desired effect, and the outline of a head and shoulders appeared from the side of the cab. Mustering all my strength, I clobbered the shadowy outline, and the body rolled out and lay motionless in the snow. I quickly stepped over it and reached for the ignition key. It started instantly and I rammed it in gear and released the clutch. Scrabbling along the row of switches, my hand found the lights, and a flood of light went up before me as the headlamps picked out the road ahead. It was snowing hard now and I had difficulty keeping the truck on the road. There were tall poles each side of the road marking the edges, and I had to slow down in order to keep them in focus. After several miles, the hypnotic effect of the poles caused my eyes to glaze over, and it took all my willpower to retain focus. I began to sink into an exhausted drowsiness, longing with every fibre in my body to just close my eyes and sleep. Suddenly the poles were closer together and angled sharply to the left. I turned the wheel, but the corner got tighter, causing me to brake hard. The truck spun and began zigzagging along as I tried to correct it. Then came a series of jolts and I clung desperately to the steering wheel as small trees loomed up in front of me. There was a noise of smashing obstacles and I was thrown sideways as the truck careered off the road. Then there was another shattering blow to the side of the truck, and after a moment of weightlessness, I found myself deposited flat on my back in deep snow for the second time that night.

After brushing off the snow I scrambled back up to the road. I didn't feel any worse than before the accident, but that wasn't saying much. But at least I was fully awake now.

Having no alternative, I trudged off along the road, knowing that I would have to find shelter soon as I was almost completely exhausted. The snow began to ease, and the moon once more tried to penetrate the gloom to assist me.

Coming to a minor track that I thought might lead to a farm, I struck off along it, summoning up all my remaining strength to push my legs forwards. At last a shape came into view that I prayed would be shelter. Past caring about caution, only two thoughts possessed me. Shelter and sleep. Just to lie somewhere dry and close my eyes and sleep was all that mattered now. Even the thought of death no longer bothered me; in fact, it would be a relief. Getting close, I saw it was an old wooden cowshed. This would do admirably.

Free of snow under the overhanging roof, I searched for the door, and seconds later I was unbolting the lower half and pushing back the sacking that hung over the top half. It smelled invitingly of warmth, fresh hay and cows, as I staggered inside and fell to the floor.

"Shit!" I swore, instantly realising the accuracy of my muttered annoyance.

Crawling forwards to find a more pleasant resting place, I felt the warmth of a calf's body. All my reserve now gone, I lay beside it and began to sink into a blissful sleep.

One final recollection came to me; it was of a cold, wet nose, followed by a sloshing noise and slimy feel of a large, wet tongue, licking my outstretched hand.

"Probably thinks I'm its mother," I murmured, smiling contentedly in the darkness of my hospice.

Chapter 3

The sound of the cowshed door, noisily scraping on the stone step as it was pulled open, brought me to wakefulness. Daylight streamed in, and through the opening came an old man. Dressed in a dark suit of thick material that hung loosely about his thin body, he moved along the line of animals, looking briefly at each one. I could see his face beneath a battered, wide-brimmed trilby, which like his suit seemed to swamp his small frame. His deeply lined face looked as though it had been carved out of the wood of an old tree.

I attempted to get up but only managed to struggle to a sitting position. The calf with whom I'd shared the night objected to my pushing, and promptly jumped up, crying out its annoyance.

The old man turned and spotted me. Pausing for a moment, he then stepped across and stood looking at me, his mask-like face betraying nothing of his feelings.

"Ich bin Anglish," I said, in Swiss-Deutsch dialect. "Kann sie helfen mir bitte?"

If he understood my plea, he didn't show it. He remained silent; his deep blue eyes fixed intently on me as he stood there.

"Mine Deutsch is schlect." I tried again. "Sprechen

sie Anglish?"

A moment's pause, then he spoke. "Ya, a little. Vos ist?"

"I am Anglander, I was in accident." He continued to look at me, not moving from where he stood, as I went on, "Do you understand, I was in AK-SEE-DENT. Verstehen sie dis?"

"Ya, verstehen sie," he said, "komm."

I took hold of his outstretched hand and felt the strength of his gnarled fingers as they gripped mine. He pulled me up with the ease of a man used to handling heavy objects A lifetime spent carrying fodder over mountains had endowed him with strength that his wizened appearance belied.

He turned, and pushing past an inquisitive cow, made for the door. I pushed past the confused animal and limped after him. Once outside, he stopped and looked back at me as I emerged.

"Kann sie valk?" he enquired.

"Ya, ya," I replied.

"Kommen sie," he said, and made off across the trodden snow path. It wasn't snowing but the cold morning caused me to shiver, and I realised how warm it had been in the cowshed. As I followed him, my stiffness began to wear off, and reaching the crest of a slight hill, he paused and beckoned me to follow. An old Walliser chalet stood in a clearing in front of a forest of tall pines. It was the type that had the living accommodation built above a cow shed that housed a dozen or so cows through the winter. Its wooden sides were black with age except where the heat generated by the animals below had filtered through the seams and bleached the woodwork above. I followed him up the steps to a little door, and moments later we stood together in the warmth of his modest home. There was an old iron stove with its metal flue pipe, disappearing through a blackened asbestos panel into the wooden roof. There were small windows that had little red and white check cotton curtains hanging from each side.

As my host walked around the solid wooden chairs and equally solid table, to a large, old dresser, I took in the rest of the room. It was like a picture from the days of the early settlers. Everything was of rough wooden construction, and around the walls were several plaques with wood carvings, and a brass oil lamp hung from a heavy chain in the centre of the ceiling.

"You like to vosh?" he asked.

Looking down at myself and realising the reason for his question, I felt uncomfortable to be standing in his home in such a state.

"Ah yes, very much, danke," I replied.

Removing my anorak, I hung it on a peg by the door, as the old man went through a narrow, timbered archway into another room. There came the sound of running water and, removing my ski boots, I went through to join him. To my surprise there was a modern bath together with a wash basin and the other usual fittings.

"Venn you finish ve have essen," he spoke hesitantly, searching for the words in English. "Here ist razor apparat." Taking a razor from a wall cabinet, he placed it on the basin and went out.

As he closed the door, I called after him, "Thank you, veilen danke."

Stripping off my clothes in front of the mirror above the basin, I stepped back to look at myself. "Jesus Christ!" I exclaimed. "What a bloody mess."

The dark stubble of my unshaven face was caked with dirt and cow dung. There was a slight swelling under my left eye and several yellow and blue bruises about my arms and body. Turning to view my back showed a similar picture, plus a swelling below my left shoulder. My arm and shoulder muscles responded stiffly to flexing at first, but after trying several times they loosened up and moved more freely. As an army PTI my favourite exercise had been repetition back planches on the horizontal bar. It was a gymnastic movement which I could still execute, and the resulting thick layers of muscle that covered my back had afforded it protection and saved me from serious injury.

I moved across to the bath and lowered myself to let the warm water engulf me. It seeped into my body and brought new life to my aching limbs.

"Komm," I called, in answer to a knock at the door, and in came the old man carrying a large towel.

He laid it on the basin and went out again.

I stepped out of the bath, and drying myself I

thanked him silently, as I felt the warmth from the towel that he'd thoughtfully warmed on the stove. I shaved and cleaned my clothes, then dressed and went through to join the old man.

At his invitation I joined him at the table, and between mouthfuls of dark Walliser bread and full fat cheese, I began explaining why I came to be there. The truth was too complicated, so I told him that I had been ski touring and lost my way. Because of the language difficulty it was necessary to keep it as simple as possible. He then produced a map and showed me that we were near the Swiss village of Saas Almagell. His eyes not seeming to move from me, he refilled my mug of black coffee from the enamel pot that stood on the table between us. Noticing that I'd eaten most of the bread and cheese, I apologised for my greediness.

"Machs nicht," he said with a nonchalant shrug, and rising from his chair, he reached up for his old trilby and made for the door.

"Arbeiten," he said, and I realised that he had work to do with his cattle. I got up to say something, but the door pulled shut with a creak and he was gone.

Alone in the old chalet I began to feel strangely uneasy. Pondering over the events of the previous day, an explanation started to take shape in my brain. Suppose I had stumbled into a smuggling ring. Contraband across the border from Italy was a well organised business, and the gang that I'd escaped from could have mistaken me for someone from the authorities. It seemed logical enough, and if it was a smuggling ring, there would be accomplices on this side of the border. What if the old man was part of it, and why did he leave so suddenly? He could be off to contact the gang.

I went over to the window and peered out from behind the curtain. It was snowing heavily, and the large flakes had already covered the old man's tracks.

Crossing to the stove, I picked up a log, and using it to open the front, I threw it in. Clanging the flap shut, I turned my back and stood enjoying its warmth.

"It's no good, I don't like it," I said to myself, "you'd best get away from here."

I grabbed my anorak and examined it. It was dry now, and I brushed it, but it was stained and the rip it had suffered hung open. It was the reversible type, so I pulled out the sleeves so that it was inside out. My blue anorak with a grey lining was now in opposite colours and what's more the rip was now on the inside. There was a small zipped pocket inside the sleeve, and on opening it I was pleased to see that the Swiss franc notes that I always carried with me were still there. Pleased with my new appearance, my spirits rose and, placing a ten franc note under the coffee pot, I put on my boots and left.

Leaving the chalet, I struck off along a path skirting the edge of the forest. The going was easier here with less snow under the overhanging trees. After about twenty minutes a small red triangle painted on the side of a fir tree confirmed that I was on a recognised path. My concern was not knowing the direction I was taking. Rounding a bend, I saw one of the 'wanderweg' signposts that mark the Swiss mountain paths. They indicate not only the direction, but also the time it will take the average hiker to reach the chosen destination. Coming close, I read 'SAAS-FEE - ¾ Stunden'.

I knew the village well and it meant that in three quarters of an hour I would be in Saas-Fee and safe. Half an hour later I was on the road that led to the village. Colourful anoraks came into view as people mingled with each other between the quaint old chalets and the more modern but architecturally matching hotels. Continuing through the narrow streets, I eyed with amusement the mixture of fashionable shops with the latest skiing fashions, rubbing shoulders with the old black chalets that still had cows housed beneath them.

A man in overalls came down the street leading a giant bull, and I paused as they turned across my path into a side alley. The bull was being led by a chain with a ring through its nose, and as it passed me it had difficulty keeping its feet on the slippery cobbles. I had never seen such a huge beast. His enormous testicles hung so low they almost touched the ground, as they swung to and fro, like a pendulum in rhythm to his laboured progress.

"I pity the poor bloody cows around here," I said. Then as an afterthought, I added, "I don't know though," grinning to myself.

As I came to the car park where all the vehicles had to stop, not being allowed in the village, an alpine restaurant caught my eye. Feeling great to be back among people, I went in and sat down at one of the empty tables. A pretty waitress came over, wearing a white blouse. It was so tight across the front it stretched the buttonholes from the vertical to the horizontal. Handing me the menu, she stood for a moment re-tying her apron behind her waist, as I scanned the card with one eye and watched the struggling blouse buttons with the other.

She scribbled down my order for Wiener schnitzel, pomme-frites and gemuse. "Fur drinken?" she asked. "Ya, flaschen bier bitte," I replied.

As she hurried away, I watched the lower cheeks of her bottom just managing to peep out from below the micro mini skirt, into which the tights that covered her ample thighs disappeared.

The sight stimulated thoughts that were far removed from my recent exploits.

When she returned with my meal, I couldn't resist taking another look at the view, as she leaned over the table next to mine, reaching for some empty glasses. Her garments stretched tightly across her round buttocks, stirring a desire within me, confirming that a man's physical condition is no barrier to his imagination.

My plate clean, I drank the last of my 'Gurten Special Hell' and motioned to the girl that I wished to pay. As she opened the purse from beneath her apron, I told her to keep the change and prepared to leave. Resisting the temptation of watching her bottom play peek-a-boo as she walked away, I rose and left the restaurant. It had stopped snowing and a group of young skiers were gathered around a pile of skis and luggage. As a yellow post bus arrived, they immediately began loading everything onto the platform at the rear, talking loudly as they jostled together. They were Americans and had obviously finished their holiday and were returning home. The bus was going to Visp so I decided to join it. From Visp it would be easy to catch a train back to Zermatt and collect my belongings from the luggage office.

Thinking about what I'd been through in the last twenty-four hours filled me with hatred towards those responsible. What had it really been about? What motive could they have had in holding me prisoner and trying to kill me? The thoughts caused me to lose some of the carefree feeling that I'd enjoyed with my new-found freedom. The only thing I knew for certain was that should I meet up with Garlic Mouth on level terms, I would teach that greasy bastard a lesson. The chances of that happening however were very thin, and in any case, alone and unarmed, it would be lunacy to try and find him. The thought of leaving the debt unpaid stung my pride, but I was forced to admit to myself that the most sensible solution was to collect my things and go on to Riederalp, leaving the mystery, and my anger, unresolved.

Buying a ticket as I boarded the bus, I pushed my way through the jungle of young skiers, smelling the perspiration and sun-tan lotion that filled the air. Emerging into a clearing at the back of the bus, I sat down on the bench seat next to a young woman. She was alone, and I noticed the plaster cast that encased her left foot and lower leg. As I sat there, she drew in her leg and smiled.

"I hope that's not too bad," I said, nodding towards her injury.

"Would you believe it?" she asked, "I've been skiing for years, and now this year I have to trip while I'm waiting for the drag lift and break my darned ankle."

I laughed, not unkindly. "Are you all off home to America?" I asked.

"No, we've had ten days here, and now we're going to Verbier for ten days more."

"That's going to be a disappointment for you, with that," I said.

Following my glance towards her plastered limb, she nodded ruefully. The bus moved off jerkily, causing us to roll together, our shoulders touching. "You look a little worse for wear yourself," she said, looking up into my face, smiling again."

"I had a little accident myself," I said, "I had an argument with a tree, and the tree won. Does it look too bad?"

"No, I didn't notice it till I looked at you closely. I guess it's a great sport if you don't weaken," she said.

Her smile widened and I found her natural warmth and open friendliness very relaxing, as I settled back for the journey.

The young skiers, some seated and others standing along the centre of the bus, carried on their jubilant conversation, as the bus continued along the twisting mountain road. Each downhill hairpin was preceded by a squeal of brakes as we approached, causing the skis on the carrier behind to clatter together noisily as we rounded a bend. A little further on, with brakes squealing loudly, we slowed up and came to a stop. Looking through the window, I saw that we'd arrived at the lower village of Saas-Grund. Two cars were drawn up at each side of the road in front of us. 'POLIZEI' was prominently painted in large letters along their sides. Several men were standing about, jackbooted and wearing thick belts over their uniforms, attached to which were ominous looking leather holsters. They looked reminiscent of an old movie portraying a scene about the German Gestapo.

I glanced at my companion, "What's this about I wonder?" I asked.

"I suppose they're looking for the hijacker," she replied disinterestedly.

"Hijacker?"

"Yes, you know, the one that attacked a soldier and stole an army truck last night," she said.

My heart leaped. "I didn't know," I murmured to her, my lips suddenly dry.

"Didn't the police visit your hotel this morning? she asked.

"No."

"That's funny, they came to ours at breakfast, and the waiter told us that they were looking for someone who'd attacked a soldier at some army post around here and stolen a truck. They found the truck smashed up down a ravine, and now they're on the lookout for whoever did it. Funny they didn't come to your hotel."

Instantly the truth hit me. Driven by fear and exhaustion, I had mistakenly imagined an army outpost as part of the gang that I was escaping from.

"I slept late, they must have come before I went down for breakfast," I lied. "What about the soldier who was attacked?"

"Oh, I think he was killed," she said.

The casualness of her reply did nothing to lessen its impact upon me. For one dreadful moment my head spun and my whole body went limp.

"Are you alright?" she asked.

"Yeh — sure — too much wine last night," I stammered. "Did they give a description of the attacker?"

She gave a wave to one of the other skiers. "I don't think they have one," she replied. "Say, I love those fondues they have here, and that Fendant wine they drink with it, don't you?"

"Yes, it's very good," I said.

What if the old farmer had reported the stranger in his cowshed? It wouldn't take long for them to piece together the two events, and they would be looking for an Englishman.

Two burly police officers entered the bus, and as one spoke to the driver, the other officer looked down the bus at its occupants. They must have been satisfied that this was a party of American tourists, as with a final word to the driver, they left.

"Hey, Miriam, did you get that ski instructor to sign your plaster — gee that guy was the handsomest though wasn't he?" One of the kids from along the bus was calling back to my young friend.

The thought that I'd killed a young soldier, while he sat having a quiet smoke, shattered me. Should I make a clean breast of it and give myself up? But who would believe my story of being attacked? I didn't even know on which side of the border it had happened. I first needed to find some proof.

I'd come looking for some excitement and a little fun, and I'd sure found the excitement. The way things had turned out wasn't funny, and I wasn't of a mind to let the Garlic Mouth gang get away with it now. No longer part of the joyful scene around me, I felt like a cornered animal, and filled with a rage at the knowledge of what my captors had driven me to. I would make them pay for it whatever the cost. As the bus lurched on around a succession of steep curves, narrowly missing the precipitous edges, a plan of revenge spawned in my brain and grew quickly in the nourishment of my vindictiveness.

Chapter 4

The bus pulled into the station at Visp, and hardly before it stopped, the excited young Americans were scrambling out and flocking to collect their skis and luggage. Helping Miriam off the bus, I escorted her to the rear to wait for her luggage to be unloaded.

"We have to catch the train to Martigny and then the coach to Verbier," she said, as I carried her gear to the platform. "There's an hour to wait."

Everyone was shuttling back and forth to the heap of belongings that were piling up against the station building. I looked about and saw a police car across the street, but no sign of its occupants.

Pausing in front of the notice board, I scanned the timetable for the next train to Brig. It wasn't due for two hours, which meant that I would be alone for an hour after the others had left. I wouldn't be vulnerable while I could mix with this group, but after that I would be conspicuous.

Miriam had disappeared into the 'Damen' side of the partitioned lavatory, so I slipped around and went to the ticket office. By getting my ticket now, I could board the train at the last moment and mix with the others that I hoped would be waiting. There were no barriers to go through as all tickets were checked on the train. If the police were watching, I could mingle with the other passengers. I joined Miriam again, and someone suggested a drink, so we all trooped across to the tearoom. I took a corner seat next to Miriam, as it gave me a clear view across to the station, through the potted plants that ranged along the windowsill. As a couple of the others shared our table, I sat enjoying a citron tea and a large slice of Schwarzwälder Torte.

"Hey fellas, the trains about due," came a shout and everyone rose en masse with much scraping of chairs and the commotion of paying. As the waitresses added up the dozens of little tickets, some of the kids began leaving, while others were bickering about who should pay for what. Those at our table settled their dues, and after giving the waitress an extra franc, I ushered Miriam towards the door. Two policemen were now sitting in the patrol car but seemed uninterested in the group of people emerging from the tearoom. Saying goodbye to Miriam, I slipped around the side of the tearoom and along the street towards the centre of the town. It was quite busy with children from school and moving about among them and the shoppers was safer than standing about on my own in the station.

A routine check would immediately reveal that I had no passport, and this would lead to my being questioned, leading to my arrest. Stopping by a newspaper kiosk, I read down the headlines of the papers to see if there was anything about the killing of a soldier. Nothing that I could translate made any mention of it. Walking on, I rounded a corner and came to the main crossroads, where two policemen were standing at the traffic lights. As I walked past, I could feel their gaze on me, causing the hairs on the back of my neck to stand up, as I waited for their challenge. Three steps further on, as I began to draw away, no shout came from them. Keeping a casual pace despite the urge to hurry, a few moments later I was mingling with the other pedestrians and soon out of sight of the police.

"Phew!" I hissed as I released my breath, "Steady Matt, don't lose your cool."

Circling the block back towards the station, I saw there were fewer people on the street. The tall buildings on either side had overhanging balconies that kept out most of the fading light, casting shadows along the pavement. Several shops had hanging signs with 'Antiquities' written on them. Old cow bells, copper pots and junk of all kinds were displayed in the windows. It was obviously the flea market part of town. A particularly old and dirty-fronted shop caught my attention, and I crossed over to take a closer look. At the back of the window were two shotguns and peering closer revealed more firearms and a motley selection of ancient pistols and revolvers.

I went in, and closing the door, I stood in the murky gloom of the musty room and stared around at the dusty shelves. Every space was crammed with relics and curiosities of all kinds. In a tall, shelved unit against the back wall, there were several old revolvers and a not too clumsy looking pistol. I picked it up and turned towards a better light to examine it. Watching me from behind the counter was a woman that I hadn't seen enter, and her sudden presence startled me. She was dressed in black and her long grey hair was drawn back, giving her a witch-like appearance.

"Ich gerne kaufen diese pistol," I said, hoping she would understand that I wanted to buy it. "Haben sie ammunition bitte?" I didn't know the Deutsch for gun or ammunition.

She shrugged her shoulders and answered me in a dialect that meant nothing.

"Bullets — haben sie bullets?" I persisted. Shaking her head and gabbling away at me, she reached forwards as if to take the gun. I avoided her outstretched hand and drew back. Turning the gun sideways, I withdrew the magazine.

"Here," I said, "Ich wunchen bullets fur hier."

She shrugged again and, muttering to herself, went back to the rear room. Several minutes passed and I could hear her rummaging about. What if she was phoning the police? If I was caught trying to purchase a gun, it would really cook my goose.

As I was about to give up and leave, she emerged carrying a small cardboard box. Handing it to me, she tried to explain something, but I couldn't understand, and I opened the box. It was full of bullets and when I tried them in the magazine they fitted perfectly. What she was trying to tell me didn't matter now. I took out my money and offered her some notes until she nodded in agreement, then pocketing the rest of the bullets, I zipped the gun into the side pocket of my ski pants. Seconds later I was hurrying away down the shadowy backstreet towards the station.

Enough people were waiting for me to mingle inconspicuously to await the train to Brig. There was no sign of the police car. Dead on time, the train came humming along the track and pulled up with the brakes squealing loudly as it stopped. I pushed forwards with the crowd, to the nearest door of a second-class carriage, and took a seat beside an elderly couple who were sitting there. Apart from nodding my head to the conductor when he clipped my ticket, I remained silently thinking about the old lady in the gun shop. Perhaps she had been trying to explain that I needed a permit in order to buy the gun and was asking to see it. Oh well, it didn't matter now, and as she'd sold it to me, she couldn't contact the police as it would incriminate her.

It was almost dark when the train pulled into Brig, and as I descended the pedestrian subway towards the main hall, it was hardly possible to distinguish one person from another in the dim light.

"Sod it!" I swore. There were two uniformed policemen by the double doors leading to the main street. I suddenly stopped and several people behind me bumped into my back, but I turned and pushed past them, ignoring their protests, as I returned under the subway and back to the platform. The train was still there, and I walked its length until the platform sloped down to the tracks. I crossed the rails and ran along beside a row of flat trucks that stood by the unloading bays on the other side. Cars using the rail service through the Lotchburg tunnel from Kandersteg were driven off here, and I knew from experience there were no formalities.

If the police were watching the station, they wouldn't expect their man to be arriving from Kandersteg, it being in the opposite direction on the other side of the Oberland range. It was a pretty safe bet that this way out would be unguarded. Flo would have staked her week's wages on it.

I was right.

Making use of every bit of cover, I was soon standing on the exit road that led to the main highway, where it curved under the bridge to the station. I felt the marked drop in temperature as I stood at the corner by the bridge. It was going to be a cold and inhospitable night.

"Well it's no good hanging about here," I said to myself, "I'm going to have to chance it".

I needed a room for the night, nothing too grand where I would stand out, but nothing too sleazy either because that would be the obvious target for police scrutiny. Being a busy centre of commerce, Brig had hotels, both large and small, which catered for top executives down to the grubbiest manual workers, so I should find one that suited me. I hurried under the bridge and along the road towards the shopping centre, and the hotels and banks that border the outskirts of the town. I turned up my collar and crossed the bridge that went over the river Rhone. Hardly more than a modest stream as it leaves Brig, it gathers strength as it runs through the valley to become the mighty river Rhone by the time it flows out from Lake Geneva, and down across southern France to the Mediterranean.

Close by, just off the road that leads to the Simplon Pass into Italy, is the old Hotel Eggishorn. Modest, but comfortable, it would be just right to provide me with a safe haven for the night. I waited for a car to pass, then ran through the slush that was building up on the road, until I came to the steps of the hotel. Knocking off my boots on the top step, I opened the door and went in. It was warm inside, and had that pleasant smell of waxed wood, so distinctive of these old Swiss hotels.

Crossing the floor of the restaurant, I made my way to the little counter by the stairs that served as the reception. There was no one about, it being too early for the evening meals, and I stood for a moment admiring the old wooden panels that gleamed in the soft light from the four wall lamps that glowed from behind their red hessian shades.

Picking up the brass bell that stood by the register, I rang it gently and waited. No one came, so I rang with more vigour, and this time a girl came hurrying along the corridor from the kitchen. Wearing open leather topped clogs, their loose wooden heels banged heavily on the floor as she came towards me. The muscles of her bare calves were the largest I had ever seen on a girl. As if not to be out done by the lower part of her body, her breasts, which swung freely from beneath a loose-fitting jumper, were also of magnificent proportions.

"Guten abend," she said pleasantly, and as she brushed past me to her position behind the counter, I felt the nearness of her body as her jumper stroked the front of my anorak.

"Guten abend," I replied, "haben sie eine zimmer fur heute abend bitte?"

She leaned forwards onto one elbow and looked at the bookings. As she did, the magnificent two rested themselves on the counter behind the register.

"Ya," she said, turning the page, "mit bad oder ohne bad?"

Thinking I should conserve my funds until I could get to the bank, "No bath," I replied, then quickly in German, "kiene bad," I repeated.

"Ah, you are English," she said, lifting her head, her large, brown eyes looking up at me.

"Yes, that's right," I said, "you speak English?"

"Yes, I was in England two years before," she answered.

I relaxed, happy to find someone with whom I could enjoy a little normal conversation. "What part of England were you in?"

She stood up and shook her long black hair back off

her face, and the movement set up a chain- reaction that resulted in a beautiful turbulence from under the jumper.

"I worked in a hotel in Bournemouth," she went on, "its lovely there, do you know it?"

"Yes," I said, "but not very well."

Our small talk continued for a while, and I found her pleasant homely manner enjoyable. Her face was plain and rather oily, but not uninviting, and somehow seemed to match the ample proportions of her body. Then I realised that I had become so mesmerised by the antics under the jumper when she moved, I had forgotten about the danger I was in. She spoke English, and if the news of the hijacked truck and the death of the soldier had been in the papers or on the radio, she might easily get suspicious when I couldn't produce any luggage. If the old farmer had given the police my description, it would be included in the news that they were looking for an Englishman.

I quickly thought of something to allay any suspicions she might have.

"I was on my way to Riederalp," I began, "but the lights on my car have failed and I've left it at a garage and walked here. I shall collect it early tomorrow morning when it's repaired."

She listened patiently, showing no signs of disbelief.

"After I've eaten, I would like to pay for everything, so that I can leave early without disturbing you, if that's alright."

"Yes of course," she said. "Will you fill in the

tourist card please?" I knew these to be obligatory so that the cantonal tax on tourists could be collected.

"I left my luggage and passport in the car," I lied, "but I know all the details, I'm used to filling them in."

After completing it with a fictitious address and passport number, I handed the pen back to her.
She smiled and turned to a row of pigeonholes behind her. Selecting a key, she turned back to me. "I will show you to your room," she said, and coming around from behind the counter, she brushed past me like before, but much closer this time. Looking into my eyes as she passed, she said quietly, "I think you will find everything you require here."

I followed her up the stairs and along the corridor. Although I preferred the view from the front, seeing her from this angle did nothing to make me lose interest. Reaching number nineteen, she unlocked the door and stood back slightly for me to enter. It was now my turn to do the brush past bit, and removing my anorak, so as not to lose any of the sensation, I moved towards her. They seemed to have grown even bigger, as I squeezed past her through the doorway, and for one beautiful moment I thought I wouldn't make it.

Once inside the room, I asked, smiling at her, "What time is dinner?"

"Any time after seven, until nine," she said, leaning back against the door frame.

The moment was interrupted by a by a loud call from someone downstairs.

"Oh, excuse me I must go," she said, and handing me the key, she hurried off down the corridor, clip clopping along on the wooden floor.

I closed the door, and removing my anorak and boots, I stretched out on the bed. Lying there on the soft eiderdown and thinking about her I became aware of a hard lump in my trousers. Unzipping the side pocket, I drew out the pistol that I'd purchased earlier. The pressure against my thigh disappeared but the lump in my ski pants remained as I closed my eyes and thought of her.

Kneeling on the bed beside me, she took hold of the jumper and pulled it over her head, then leaned across so that her breasts hung down above me. Gradually she lowered them down until their heavy softness engulfed my head and chest. I felt her hand reach down and take hold of me as she lifted one leg over mine and moved her whole body into close contact with me. The blood pounded through my veins, and every fibre within me was vibrating down to the nerve ends. Our bodies merged as she drew me in, pressing down onto me with crushing weight. The rhythmic movement of her body heightened the pressure on my chest, crushing out the breath within it.

The top of my head exploded, and a loud noise hammered in my ears. "Herr Jones! Herr Jones!"

I leaped up from the bed as the loud hammering continued. "Herr Jones, wunchen sie essen?"

It was a woman's voice, and she continued to bang

noisily on the door, calling out the name I had written on the tourist card.

"Ya — ya, ich komm sofort," I shouted in alarm, leaning against the bed to regain my composure after being awakened so suddenly from my dream.

"Sie haben tzehn minuten," came the voice again.

"Danke — danke — ich kommen."

She went away.

"Christ, what a dream that was," I panted, and wondered how long it had been since I'd experienced that sort of dream. "Not since I was fourteen, I guess," I said, grinning to myself.

After hiding the gun under the mattress, I went down to the restaurant. The clock at the bottom of the stairs struck nine as I entered the dining room. There was a table in the corner set for one, and as I reached it and sat down, 'Titsalina' came across.

"I asked madame to call you in case you were sleeping and missed dinner," she said, brushing her hair back from one cheek.

"Thanks, I probably would have," I said, looking up at her and confirming that my dream had not exaggerated their size.

Giving her my order, I watched as she hurried off towards the kitchen, then settled back and took stock of my surroundings. The restaurant was empty except for a middle-aged, balding man studying the contents of his briefcase that were spread out on the tablecloth. Sipping a coffee and shuffling through the documents, he never looked up. I took him to be a commercial traveller totting up the day's business. Pulling out the rolled newspaper from its stand close to my table, I unwound it from the wooden pole and examined each page for any report of a manhunt. There was nothing that I could recognise, and no glaring headlines about a wanted Englishman. Perhaps it came too late for the papers. I replaced it in the stand as 'Titsalina' returned with the food. Wishing me 'Guten appetite', she left me to enjoy it.

Finishing my meal, I drank the last of the wine and then went across to the counter. 'Titsalina' had returned there and had been watching me, as she stood cleaning off imaginary dust from the already polished surface.

Putting down the cloth, she asked, "Have you finished your meal?"

"Yes, thank you," I said, "and I'd like to pay for everything now, so that I can leave early in the morning."

"You don't want breakfast?"

"No thank you."

She leaned across the counter towards me, this time wearing a blouse instead of the jumper, her nipples pushing into the silken material as the almost see-through fabric stretched to their outline. Adding up the bill she handed it to me, and gripping her fingers, she returned my squeeze.

It was the encouragement I needed. "Is everything included?" I asked, stressing the word 'everything'.

Her large brown eyes looked at me as she smiled.

"Yes, I have included the room, meal, taxes and service. That is everything, unless you require something more." She paused, then went on. "I go off duty very soon, and the restaurant and kitchen will be closed."

"Do you live here in the hotel?" I asked quickly.

"Yes, I have a room on the top floor," she replied, still smiling.

"Then could you bring a bottle of Henniez to my room, on your way up later?"

The question was loaded, as she knew that I could quite easily have taken it with me now.

She didn't hesitate. "Of course, I will be about twenty minutes, will that be okay?" Her large brown eyes searched mine for acknowledgement.

"Yes, that will be fine," I replied. "Shall I pay now?"

"No — later." The smile she gave me could only mean that my proposition had been accepted.

Back in my room, I removed the gun from under the mattress, zipped it into my anorak pocket and hung the anorak with the pocket turned inwards, on the back of the bedroom door. As I turned away a little ditty came to my head, and I chanted it to myself as I danced around the bed.

"Her calves were huge, her hair was long, my God you should have seen her. Her boobs were like two rugby balls and I called her Titsalina."

Moving across to the window, I turned off the light and stood looking through the curtains at the snow-packed car park below. The wrought iron electric lamps shone down, revealing it to be empty except for a solitary Volkswagen. Its beetle shape was covered with several inches of snow, and I guessed it belonged to the commercial traveller.

Looking at my watch by the light from the window, I saw there were only ten minutes to wait. I began to thrill at the thought of what was ahead for me. The thought of sex had drugged me into forgetting all else.

The noise of a car sounded, as a pair of headlights shot through the snow and entered the hotel entrance. As it stopped and the occupants got out, I glimpsed the word painted along its side.

'POLIZEI'.

I was across the room to the door, and had my anorak on, before I realised what I'd done. "Hang on a second," I whispered, steadying myself, "don't rush — just think for a minute."

I thought it over. It was possible that they had come in for a coffee to have a break from their night duty. But then she had told me that the restaurant was closing. Maybe she had tipped them off that a lone Englishman, with no papers or luggage, was staying here. On the other hand, it could just be a routine visit, and a regular part of their shift, when they had a schnapps to keep out the cold.

I didn't want to sacrifice my night with 'Titsalina' if she was on the level with me, but neither could I afford to be caught, especially as I was in possession of a gun.

My mind made up, I opened the bedroom door and crept quietly along the passageway to a glass panelled door at the end. The key was in the lock, and turning it silently, I opened the door and went out onto the stone steps that led down to the road. I hurried off in the direction of the Simplon pass, keeping to the shadows that provided me with cover. Worried that my tracks could be followed from the hotel, I walked through the slush on the road that had been created by the traffic. As the cold began to penetrate my anorak, I thought about my missed appointment back in my room.

"Of all the rotten luck," I muttered, "fancy those sods turning up now."

I shrank down into my upturned collar, and pushed both hands deeper into my pockets, my left-hand tightening on the pistol. My frustration and anger heightened, as did my resolve to get even with Garlic Mouth. Trudging on, I realised it was going to be a bloody miserable night, and after such promise too!

There was no wind, and the snow deadened every sound, except the quiet shuffling of my footsteps. The lamps had disappeared behind me, but there was still enough light filtering through the night for me to distinguish shapes and outlines, as my eyes adjusted to the gloom. Coming to a railway crossing, I crossed, knowing that there would be workman's huts alongside the tracks. I had seen them at intervals when I'd travelled by train. If I could find one it would provide shelter for the night. I followed the rails, listening for any train that might be approaching. Powered by the overhead electric cables, these trains were almost silent, and I didn't fancy a ride on the front snowplough that they attached in winter. They would be running all night as the Swiss made sure that their train service wasn't halted by snow.

Peering ahead it wasn't long before I saw the dim outline of a hut looming in front of me. Locating the door, I fumbled around for the handle, and breathed a sigh of relief as it turned, and the door opened.

Groping around, I found a light switch but hesitated at the thought of switching it on. Calculating that there wouldn't be anyone near enough to see it, I switched it on. I was standing in a small shed about twelve feet square and empty except for some tools and other items of equipment. In the corner there were poles that were used as snow markers, and a collection of oilskins hanging from a peg by the small window. Closing the door, I took one of the oilskins and draped it over the window, and the others would make me a rough bed. Putting out the light and uncovering the window, I felt my way into the stiff bedclothes and settled down for the night. Telling myself that I must be away early, before any workmen arrived, it was soon obvious that I wouldn't oversleep through being too comfortable.

With thoughts of what 'Titsalina' would be thinking, if in fact the police visit had been nothing to do with me, my exhaustion soon overcame the discomfort of the hard bed, and within a short time I was sound asleep.

Chapter 5

Cold and stiff, I awoke to a grey dawn. It had stopped snowing but there had been several inches during the night. Too early to start out, I settled down to wait on the pile of oilskins that had served as my bed and waited. I felt cold and hungry but at least I was free to carry out my plan.

At last it was time to go, and leaving the hut as I'd found it, I closed the door and kicked the snow about to disguise my footprints as I walked away. Braving a couple of handfuls of snow in my face to liven me up, I made off along the tracks that led back to the road. Walking briskly and keeping a watchful eye for any signs of the police, I headed for the town. It was just after nine when I arrived, and I was pleased to see that there was enough activity in the streets for me to mingle unobserved.

A little tearoom patisserie was doing brisk business with a gang of Italian construction workers, and two lorries stood by the pavement, as the workers took an early drink and noisily bought their goodies for the day. It couldn't be better, and I was soon enjoying hot coffee and a plate of assorted pastries. Going to the washroom, I smartened myself up before I left, and then made off towards one of the large buildings at the corner of the crossroads by the station. Walking up the wide granite steps, I came to the iron framed doors, above which was the large-lettered sign that showed SWISS BANK CORPORATION, and went in.

Some years ago, I had opened an account here with thoughts of buying a holiday apartment. I had decided against it but kept the account for use during my holidays. I grinned as I remembered opening the numbered account which had been so easy, and not at all the exclusive facility that was believed to be only available to millionaires or international tax dodgers.

I always dealt with the young manager, Herr Eyer, who spoke perfect English, and knew me from my regular visits. Compared to the fuss that British banks make over currency transactions, it was always very easy to draw out any amount here. With just a firm handshake, as is customary before business, he would type out a withdrawal invoice for the stated amount. Then, after my signature, he would count out the notes and pass them to me. It was as easy as that.

Looking through the glass partition, I couldn't see him there this morning. It needed to be him this time, as I had no means of proving my identity, and just signing my signature probably wouldn't be enough.

A young clerk came from the rear to deal with me, as I went to the speaking hole. "Darf ich sprechen mit Herr Eyer, bitte?" I asked, praying he wasn't on holiday or sick.

Then to my relief, "Ja, eine moment bitte," came the reply.

Picking up the intercom and pressing a couple of digits, he spoke quickly into it.

Waiting there, I glanced around the wall at the notices advertising the latest interest rates. I had only managed to read one when a door at the back opened and through it came the familiar figure of Herr Eyer. Recognising me, he came over, and lifting the glass partition, he smiled and held out his hand.

We shook hands and exchanged greetings.

"I would like to make a withdrawal," I told him.

"Certainly, Mr Sands, how much do you require?"

"Five thousand francs please," I replied.

"Yes, one moment please," he said, and taking a duplicated form, he inserted it into a typewriter and quickly rattled off the necessary details. Taking it with him through to the back office, he returned a minute later and came to the counter again. He pushed the form across to me and after checking it, I signed my name and number, and pushed it back.

"How would you like the notes?" he enquired.

"Two one thousand, four five hundred and the rest in hundreds please."

He nodded. A large drawer by his side glided open to his touch, and from various compartments he produced the notes and counted them out in front of me. He pushed them across, and I zipped the two one thousand notes into the back pocket of my ski pants and folded the rest and put them into my anorak.

Shaking hands again, we exchanged farewells, and shortly afterwards I was outside and making for the Migros supermarket and stage two of my plan.

"That was painless," I said out loud. "Let's hope the rest goes as well."

The Migros had the usual selection of shoppers, mainly women and many of them Italian speaking and probably the wives of the immigrant workers. Everyone looked drab and I wasn't conspicuous among them. The clothing section of the store was well stocked, and I found a smart anorak, and trousers in my size, together with other items including shirts, underclothes and socks. A new pair of gloves and woollen hat completed my purchases. As I pushed the trolley towards the checkout, I picked up a canvas holdall and joined the queue.

I wondered if the girl would look at me with suspicion when she checked my purchases, as it was possible they had been warned to look out for such a shopper. It was too late to put anything back; my pulse quickened as I began unloading the trolley.

Without a question, she merely looked for the price tags, and then mechanically rang them up on the till. I handed her a note to cover the tally and she put it in the till and moments later my change came down a metal chute into the metal cup at the end. Scooping it up, I pushed my purchases into the holdall and went out. Not a word or even a glance had passed between us. She was simply a bored operator sunk into a kind of mechanical monotony, and probably couldn't describe one of the hundreds of people that she checked out every day.

Hurrying away from the store, I crossed the road and headed for the public toilets and stage three.

Once inside the door with the outline of a man on it, I washed and then went into the WC and set about changing. Everything fitted well and the smell of the newness was a big improvement to what I'd been wearing. Transferring the money and gun into my new attire, I stuffed the discarded clothing into the holdall and went out to the wash basins to inspect myself in the mirror.

"Not too bad — not too bad at all," I said. It wasn't quite Saint Moritz or Gstaad, but it was fashionable enough to pass without a second glance at any of the less fashionable resorts.

As I headed back to the station for the train to Zermatt my spirits rose, and I felt quite elated.

As I reached the square in front of the station, a row of carriages stood on the tracks, under the canopy that offers the waiting passengers some protection from the winter weather. The railway ran through the main street of Brig at this point, before entering the railway cutting.

Three buses were drawn up alongside the carriages, and scores of people, obviously on a package holiday, were transferring to the Zermatt train for the last part of their journey. I should have enough time to purchase a ticket and get back to find a seat in an unreserved compartment before this lot sorted themselves out. It wouldn't be long now before I was in Zermatt, and once I had my passport again, being stopped would not present the danger that I was in now, with no means of identity.

The thought had hardly left me, when four young uniformed policemen came around the first of the buses and swaggered along towards me. If this was an identity check I was a dead duck!

The leading pair called to the driver, who opened his window and leaned out to speak to them. The other two walked on, turned between the next bus and disappeared. This was my chance. Reaching the space between the bus at my end and the next one down, I turned into the gap and hurried through. As I emerged, one of the policemen came around and we almost collided. We then proceeded to perform that comedy routine, where two people, eager to pass each other, step sideways together and then back together, still blocking each other's 'way.

"Entschuldigen," I said, and not waiting for his response, walked boldly off to the first of the two taxis that were parked opposite. Reaching the cab unchallenged, I opened the rear door and got in.

The driver put down the newspaper he was reading and turned to enquire about my destination.

"Heliport bitte," I told him.

He nodded his understanding and started the engine. The Mercedes moved smoothly away from the station

74

to join the main road.

The heliport was a small landing space marked out beside an office building. A pair of red helicopters stood there, one covered with a canvas tea cosy that only left the large blade on top exposed. The other one had someone sitting inside the cockpit and looked ready for take-off.

Paying off the taxi, I went through the glass sliding doors to the office, and approached the window marked 'Buro'. This helicopter service specialised in taking skiers to destinations in the Alps, and up to the glaciers that because of their altitude can be skied all year. A request for a flight to Zermatt would not be unusual, and as far as the police were concerned, they wouldn't expect any suspect they were looking for to have the money for a helicopter, if they needed to steal a truck.

A slim, young fellow in snappy dress accepted my order without query and moved over to the radio transmitter on the next desk. Flicking the switches, he spoke to someone at the other end, then turned on his platform heels and came back to me at the window.

"It will be about ten minutes, sir. If you would care to wait, there's a seat there and I will make out your flight ticket," he said.

Seated in the leather and chrome chair that he'd indicated, I heard the whine of the helicopter engine as the pilot began the warm-up procedure. A throb of excitement pulsed through me as I realised that within a short time, I would have my passport and luggage back.

I could then carry out my plan to get even with the bastards who had been the cause of my predicament. A strong feeling of hatred flared up inside me, as I sat there silently recalling what I had suffered at their hands. Regret about the soldier swept over me again, and I was lost in revengeful brooding, as a voice from the Buro window penetrated my thoughts.

"I have your ticket here, sir, and your flight's now ready." The smartly dressed young clerk pushed the slip of paper across the counter towards me, as I rose, picked up my canvas holdall containing my old clothes, and went to the window.

I took out a bundle of franc notes and paid him. His fancy gold bracelet brushed the counter as he counted the money and gave me the change. "If you will follow me, sir, I will take you through to your flight," he said, smiling.

He opened the door at the end of the counter, and an adjoining door that led through to the departure lounge. Opening the outer door of the lounge, he stood back for me to go out.

"The pilot will see you aboard — I hope you enjoy your trip," he said, holding the door so that it protected him from the rush of cold air that came through. He obviously didn't fancy chancing his snazzy trousers and platform shoes outside in the snow.

"Thanks," I said, and ran across to the open cockpit, where the pilot leaned out and took my holdall.

As I climbed in, he shouted a greeting above the

noise of the engine and pushed the flight ticket I gave him under a clip at the side of the cabin.

The little chopper had seats for five passengers, but being the only one, I accepted his invitation and clambered in next to him. Dressed in a red all-in-one flying suit, he was pleasant-featured and had the bronzed, athletic look of a young skier, typical of the young bloods who show off their skills on the higher slopes. He operated the controls while carrying on a two-way conversation over the intercom, and I watched his nonchalant expertise with some envy as I sat there. The noise from the engine increased as the whirling blade above us speeded up, and the little machine gently lifted off and started to gain height.

Reaching the low cloud ceiling, we continued upwards through the swirling mist, and seconds later we came out above in brilliant sunshine. As we swung around to take course, I could see the top of the cloud hanging over Brig, and beyond that the river Rhone, which wound its way along the valley. To the south I recognised the railway and tumbling stream that stretched away in front of us as we followed the same direction towards Zermatt.

"The weather's good up there," the pilot shouted, "skiing should be perfect for the next few days."

"I hope you're right," I called back.

I turned away to take in the view, and as conversation was difficult with the noise of the engine, I remained silent. Buzzing along, we followed the railway and were soon overtaking the train that I had attempted to catch earlier. It looked like a child's toy, as it wriggled along through the rocky slopes and ravines, among the mountains. Pretty soon we were approaching the familiar outline of Zermatt. We swung in over the ice rink by the station, circled the landing pad close by, then gently landed between two other choppers that were parked there.

The whirling blade lost momentum and slopped around, as the crescendo of noise slackened, and following the pilot's example, I prepared to extricate myself from the cockpit. We shook hands and he thanked me as he took the note that I offered him.

"Have a drink," I said, "thanks for a good trip."

"I'm glad you enjoyed it," he replied, "and I hope you enjoy some good skiing."

We walked together across to the reception building and with a wave we parted company, and I made off towards the station luggage room. It was six minutes to twelve and this just gave me time to collect my things before it closed for lunch. It was a different clerk, so I described my valise, and with a twenty franc note as a prompter, he found it and brought it to me. Checking it was all there, I grabbed the two bags that I now had, and hailed the driver of the carriage that stood outside. It was the one from the Grand Hotel, and the driver jumped down to collect my bags. With me aboard the rig, he barely had time to jump up in front and take up the reins before the two horses, sensing they were going back for lunch, broke into a canter.

We tobogganed along as the driver tried to restrain the galloping animals, but it wasn't until we were about to turn into the hotel entrance that he managed to bring them back to an impatient trot.

As we slithered to a halt outside the main doors, a uniformed attendant hurried out to help me down. Touching his peaked cap with a white gloved hand as I alighted, he went off in front of me to open the double swing doors that led to the foyer, while the stagecoach driver followed along with my luggage.

At the reception desk the clerk gave me his immediate attention, and twigging my accent, he replied in perfect English to my request for a room. The Grand Hotel is the most expensive in Zermatt, but now I had the money to afford it, that didn't matter. In any case it might be my last stay anywhere, and I was determined to enjoy the best on offer and was in no mood to be counting the cost.

Another uniformed flunky carried my two grips as he escorted me via the lift to my room. After accepting my tip, with the nonchalant gratitude he'd practised a thousand times, he transferred the key to the inside, closed the door and was gone.

I went through into the large, well-appointed bathroom, and as I removed my clothes, I began another conversation with myself. "From now on it's my turn to do the chasing, and Garlic Mouth and his cronies will be in for a bloody shock before long."

As I lay soaking in the hot bath, massaging my bruised muscles, my thoughts about the revenge I was planning began to trouble me. If I found Garlic Mouth and confronted him — what then?

Even if I was able to force him to surrender and accompany me to the authorities, I couldn't prove anything. He wouldn't admit to my accusations, it was only my word against his. Unless he happened to already be wanted by the police, they wouldn't act on my word alone. I would also be placing myself in their hands and would face charges of theft and manslaughter at least.

"I'm going anyway, even if it fails, I owe it to that soldier." I paused, then continuing talking to myself, went on. "Whichever way it turns out it won't help him though, poor sod."

The anger returned to my tormented mind, and the longing for revenge, illogical though it was, possessed me with such force, it wouldn't be quelled by any amount of reasoning. I had never run away from a fight, even when the odds were stacked against me, and I was' dammed if I'd start now.

Tomorrow I would get some skis and binoculars and set out to find that hut again. With maps of the area, it should be possible to locate the chalet that I'd fled from, and after that I would play it by ear.

But that was for tomorrow.

Now, after some rest, this evening would be free to enjoy dinner and a bottle of fine wine, and whatever else

I could find to amuse myself. With that in mind I finished my bath, dried myself off, and then slipped naked into bed, where I was soon lost in a deep, therapeutic sleep.

It was a little before seven when I went down, and leaving the foyer, I half fell down the three steps leading to the bar. I went in and groped my way along to a bar stool. The shadowy figure behind the bar took my order for Noilly Pratt and Henniez, and the sound of the chinking ice helped me locate the glass, as he stood it on the counter. "What the hell's the matter with this place — is the power off or something?" I asked.

As if to answer my question, a deafening noise pierced the darkness and simultaneously coloured lights began flashing on and off, as a score of youngsters got up from the tables that were now visible and began gyrating.

"Christ Almighty, what a racket!" I complained, picking up my glass and feeling half of it spill, as I tripped on the bottom step on my way out. "I need some distraction, but a bloody disco is the last thing I need right now," I grumbled, walking back to the foyer.

The desk clerk was still there, and clutching what was left of my drink, I approached him.

"Is there a quieter bar in this hotel?" I asked, the bad temper sounding in my voice.

"Yes sir, along the corridor at the other side of the restaurant."

"Thanks."

I reached the door, and immediately I entered I was cheered up by the prospect.

The lighting was normal, the air was still and quiet, and the distraction I needed was sitting at the bar.

She was dressed in a tailored green suit that contrasted effectively with her reddish-brown hair, and fitted perfectly, and what it fitted looked perfect.

This was more like what an evening at the Grand should be.

We were the only two here, as it was probably a little early for the other guests to come down.

Sinking what was left in my glass as I reached the bar, I ordered another from the pale-faced character that hovered behind it. He was wearing dark glasses, which either meant he thought it gave him an air of mystery, or he was usually in the other bar.

Miss Perfect glanced towards me and I gave her a smile. "Guten abend," I said politely.

She turned full face. "Hello," she answered, as she changed over her crossed legs, and hooked one onto the leg of the stool.

I moved nearer along the bar. "Can I offer you an aperitif, your glass looks to be empty?" I asked.

She looked at her watch before replying, and from her expression there seemed to be something troubling her. "Well, all right — thank you — actually I'm waiting to meet someone, but he hasn't turned up yet," she said.

From the States, probably in her late twenties, she would have my vote for Miss World any day.

"What'll it be?" I asked.

Oh, I'll have the same as you I think," she answered.

The pale-faced wonder behind the bar was still hunting along the row of bottles, to complete my drink, having so far only managed to get some ice into the glass.

"Bitte — die drinken — zwei," I called, and when he looked, I repeated, "zwei drinken bitte."

"Yes, sir, I will bring you two," he said, his voice deliberate, to let me know that he spoke my language better than I spoke his.

"And a slice of citron — that is lemon in each," I threw back.

I turned to Miss Wonderful. "If ever he finds the right bottle in those sunglasses, I'll lay you eight to five that when he slices the lemon, we'll finish up with two of his fingers for stirrers," I said.

She laughed, and her tanned face softened, and her body seemed to relax.

Moving closer, I dragged my stool along towards her, managing to judge the distance just right, so that our knees touched as I re-perched.

The nearness of her started to arouse that same old feeling again, as I caught a whiff of the delicate perfume she was wearing. The cut of her hair, this close, revealed that whoever styled it knew their haute coiffure. She was stunning and I forgot my troubles. "Have you been in Zermatt long?" I enquired.

"Only a few days," she said.

"Done much skiing yet?" I went on.

"No, not really — but I'm hoping to," she said, fidgeting on her stool.

"The snow is perfect now," I persisted. "You shouldn't miss it while these conditions last. Do you have much longer left of your stay here?"

The drinks came, and while paying him, I noticed that he still had all his fingers, and despite the sunglasses he had made up the right combinations.

"Cheers," I said, holding out my drink.

She picked up the other glass and chinked it against mine. "Cheers," she answered.

"I was asking how long you'll be here," I went on. "Perhaps we could do some skiing together. I know this area very well and could show you some of the best runs. Don't worry if you're not an expert, there are several very good long runs that aren't too difficult."

She was about to answer when several other people entered the bar. One was a man, not unlike me in build, and sporting the same type of shortish haircut. He was clean shaven and without a moustache.

He stood for a moment and looked over at us. Then he turned and walked to a table in the corner, by a massive cheese plant that covered the wall and was doing its best to hide the beam as well.

"I'm sorry, but you'll have to excuse me," she said, and getting off the stool, she began walking towards his table. Pausing, she turned to me and smiled. "Thanks for the drink, I'll have to return it sometime, and I'll have

84

to take a rain check on the skiing."

Did I imagine it or was there a hint of eastern promise in the look she gave me before she turned away and continued towards his table? Her figure moved like poetry in motion, and the tailored jacket emphasised the neatness of her waist and the firm but feminine swell of her buttocks.

The bar began filling, and the groups of people standing around hid them both from my view.

There didn't appear to be any unescorted females of the right age group among the new arrivals, and the chances of getting a refill from wonder boy weren't good, now that this lot were demanding his attention, so I left the bar and went along to the restaurant.

The head waiter seated me at a table for two and removed the other place setting. The tables opposite, were set for bigger numbers and looked resplendent with their starched white tablecloths and silver centre pieces holding the floral decorations. The service was good, the meal excellent, and the wine intoxicating. Miss World and her companion were sitting at a table just inside the door. His seat was facing towards me, and several times as I looked up, I caught him staring at me. Perhaps he was the jealous type and saw me as a threat. She had told me that she was waiting for someone, not anyone special like a husband, so the game was open to all-comers, and I fancied another try. He looked like a pretty tough handful if the going got tough, but the more I drank, the less formidable the opposition appeared. By the time that I'd finished the bottle they had left the dining room. I didn't exactly stagger out, but I could feel the alcohol's effect. It never usually affected me in the legs, and I put it down to my previous bird man antics. Going back to the bar there was no sign of them anywhere.

I managed to catch the eye of the sunglass kid, and he was quicker on the draw this time, as he brought me a brandy.

He forgot to bring me the change from the twenty-franc note I gave him. I tried to catch his eye again and jog his memory, but he was too busy to take any notice. I stood for a while casting my eyes over the crowd, for any unattached females that looked promising, but decided it wasn't my night and went up to bed.

Chapter 6

I woke late. The sun was already above the mountains and streaming in through the window.

"Damn, I wanted to get an early start today," I cursed, walking through to the bathroom.

By the time I went down for breakfast most of the other guests had finished theirs and left. I detest hurrying the first meal of the day, but I had to curtail my usual lingering. I hoped that I might bump into Miss World again as I returned to my room, but I was out of luck.

Back in my room, I donned my anorak and got ready to leave. Taking the lift down, I left my key at the desk and went out.

Purchasing all the things I needed took longer than I expected. I had to wait for the bindings to be fitted to the new skis I bought, so I used the time to add a pair of touring skins, a haversack and sleeping bag, four cans of beer, some chocolate and a pair of binoculars. As an afterthought I purchased a powerful rubber covered flash lamp to complete the things that I would need for the day and night ahead. Hurrying back to the hotel, I asked the doorman to take my skis and sticks to the ski room, then went to my room. After checking all the items, I went down in time for lunch.

The dining room was almost empty, but she was one of the few diners present, sitting at the same table as the night before, but alone. Dressed in a pale blue sweater and ski pants to match, she looked delicious. As I drew level, she finished her coffee and got up to leave.

"Hello again," I began, pausing at her table, "perfect day for the slopes, are you going up?"

"Not today," she answered politely, "I'm afraid I have other things to do."

She walked towards the door. "Goodbye," she said.

"That's what you call a brush off," I said with a nod to myself, "Oh well, perhaps it's for the best, I've got other things to do as well."

By the time I'd eaten lunch and consumed a drei detsi of the house wine, it was well into the afternoon. Returning to my room, I packed all the items that I'd bought earlier, plus an extra jumper and the pistol, and after collecting my skis made off to the station.

I just made it in time for the train up to Gornergrat, which would give me time to take the last lift up to the Stockhorn. Arriving there, I waited for the other skiers to make off on the ski runs back down. Then I struck off towards the peak. At the top I could see my previous route, and taking a deep breath, "Well, here goes," I said, "I hope to Christ you know what you're doing." With that I surveyed the vast, empty, snowy wilderness, and pushed off downhill.

As I plunged steeply downwards, I seemed to be

travelling faster than before and almost fell when attempting to turn. The snow had settled and was less powdery, forcing me to make wider angles.

Making a traverse, it left me with a longer climb than I'd intended. I undid the haversack, and kicking a cradle in the snow, I pulled out the climbing skins and fitted them to my skis for the trek.

This done and the pack refastened, it took a minute of struggling to get it comfortably shouldered again, and I realised that it was this extra weight that had affected my descent. The sun had dropped below the peaks as I recognised my previous route and hurrying, I rounded the mountain and saw the hut below me. I stopped and removed the skins, and having tied them around my waist, I skied on down the slope. Reaching the hut, I removed my skis and pushed open the door, realising it was going to be a long cold wait until morning. After dumping my gear, I went back out and brought in my skis. Provided the weather remained fine, I would need to get started early in order to search the area below the tree line for the chalet. The forecast had been good, but mountain weather can quickly change. Standing in the twilight, it occurred to me that should this happen, I could be stuck up here for days, making me wish that I'd brought more provisions.

"Oh well, it's too late to worry about that now," I said, and began to prepare the sleeping bag in what little light was left.

I closed the door and settled down to wait. The time

dragged slowly and eating some chocolate I took off my boots and anorak, then climbed into the sleeping bag and tried to sleep.

I woke, heart thumping, with my normally slow heart rate accelerating rapidly. High altitude can cause heart flutter, but this wasn't that kind of sensation, and I felt nervously excited.

Then came the noise.

A dull scraping sound, so faint, I lay wondering if I'd imagined it.

Then it came again, louder this time, causing the thumping in my chest to rev up even faster.

Something or someone was outside!

In one panicky movement I was out of the sleeping bag and crouching on the floor, feeling for the torch and gun.

The scraping noise came again, much louder and moving along the outside of the hut towards the door! My hand found the haversack, and feeling inside, I remembered that I'd put the torch and gun into one of my ski boots.

By the time that I'd found my ski boot and crept across with the gun, the noise had stopped, but the pounding of my heart continued so loud, I felt sure anyone outside would hear it. As the seconds ticked by, I began to wonder if it was merely an animal searching for food.

Next the noise was at the door, and my grip on the gun tightened in readiness to intercept whatever was there.

The door began to open, and shafts of moonlight pierced the darkness of the hut. Then, with a sudden jerk it burst inwards, revealing the silhouette of a figure framed in the doorway.

"Don't move or I'll shoot!" I shouted.

The figure hesitated for a moment, then half turned and fell full length towards me.

I was left looking down at the motionless figure, clearly outlined in the moonlight that flooded in.

Composing myself, I stepped over it, and stood looking at the high, white mountains and deep, shadowy valleys that stretched away in bleak isolation. Straining my eyes and ears, not a sound came through the stillness.

Satisfied I was alone except for my prostrate visitor, I pocketed the gun and bent to examine the body.

Bundled up in a thick anorak, his skis had jammed in the doorway. It took several minutes to untangle and release them before I could pull the body fully into the hut.

By the light of my torch I rolled the body over and removed the hat and goggles. He was a youngish fellow, about thirty I guessed; his eyes were closed and there was a thin trickle of blood from his nose.

"Probably got that when he hit the floor," I said, "but what the hell was he doing up here anyway?"

My thoughts raced on. Was he part of the other lot? Surely, he couldn't be looking for me. How could they possibly know that I would come back here?

I knelt closer and undid his anorak. Shining the torch inside revealed he was wearing a shoulder holster and revolver, strapped across his jumper. Reaching in to examine it, I felt the warm stickiness of the wool. Pulling the jumper up revealed that his shirt and underclothes were soaked in blood. It didn't take long to establish that he'd been shot and badly wounded. I wasn't an expert in gunshot wounds, but it seemed that a bullet had entered just above the pelvis on his right side and come out just below the ribs. "Poor sod!" I exclaimed. "No wonder you fell through the door."

Straightening up, I felt calm and confident. Gone was the sensation of panic and my heart had resumed its normal action. I checked his pulse; he was still alive, but wouldn't be for much longer, if something wasn't done quickly to stop the bleeding.

"A bloody fine boy scout you are," I grumbled to myself, "with no first aid kit or pocketknife or anything."

I searched about with the torch but there was nothing in the hut. Finally, I decided I would have to use my sleeping bag. "That's if you can tear it up," I answered my thoughts.

Attempting to tear it was hopeless as I couldn't get the seams to budge. Fixing the torch so that the beam shone on it, I wedged a ski against the wall and rubbed the seams up and down along its edge.

Soon I had enough lengths about four inches wide to make some rough bandages.

Taking hold of his shoulders, I dragged him to the

side and propped him up into a sitting position.

Examining his wound again, I knew I would have to stop the bleeding, or he would bleed to death.

I was hampered by the torch, which wouldn't stay at the correct angle for me to see what I was doing.

I removed the shoulder holster and pulled his clothes up around his head. Undoing his trousers, I saw there was another belt, and adjusting the torch I could see it was a money belt. The leather through the buckle was soaked in blood, and stubbornly refused to undo. Managing at last to expose his waist to full view, I made two pads and placed one each side of the bullet wounds. Then, using the rest of the strips, I bound them tightly into position. Covering the rough bandages with his clothes, I used the shoulder holster strap to buckle across him, in the hope that I'd stopped the bleeding.

It was the best I could do in the circumstances, and on checking his pulse again it was faint, but regular. "Good," I said.

Finally, to make him as comfortable as possible, I rolled up the rest of the sleeping bag and placed it behind him. Putting my spare jumper behind his head, I lowered him back and tied its sleeves across his chest, and then replaced his hat.

"That's the best I can do for you old son, I only hope it's good enough."

I picked up the money belt and unzipped the pocket and pulled out the contents. Folded together were four five hundred Swiss franc notes, and a bundle of Italian lira. There was also a thin leather notecase. Flipping it open, I saw a small photograph of the man I'd just bandaged, stuck to an identity card. The three imprinted words across the top met my eyes, as I held the torch closer to make sure.

I wasn't mistaken. The words 'Central Intelligence Agency' were clearly visible.

There was an official stamp and various numbers and details. My wounded companion was nothing less than a fully-fledged member of the CIA!

"What am I involved in for Christ's sake?" I uttered, as my brain digested this information.

I couldn't quite make out the small print, but beneath the photo was the name John Wallace.

Turning the card over, there was something written in pencil. It was faint from the abrasion that leather wallets cause to their contents, but I could see it was the numbers 7.12.82.

The events of the past few days came crowding back to my mind, and it was apparent that I had stumbled into something big and international. This was more than a skirmish with a few mountain villains, this was big league stuff and I was in it up to my neck. Maybe I'd been mistaken for this guy and that was why I was attacked. It would certainly explain a lot.

The more I thought of it, the more sense it made. That's why I'd been interrogated and threatened; it had to be the answer. But what had brought a member of the CIA to this remote area of northern Italy and

Switzerland? Only two possibilities came to mind, international currency smuggling or drugs. The stakes involved in both these activities were certainly high enough for the people involved to stop at nothing. The way this chap was shot up proved they were prepared to go all the way.

I shone the torch back on the CIA man. The bleeding from his nose had stopped but he showed no signs of regaining consciousness. A soon as it was light-enough I would have to make it back to Zermatt and get help.

Then I thought about what that would mean. How would I explain what I'd been doing up here, in the middle of the night with a man who'd been shot? And another thing, as far as I knew this hut could be on the Italian side, so the Swiss would be reluctant to get involved. Furthermore, it would mean revealing myself as the one responsible for the soldier's death. I was in a hell of a fix, but I couldn't just leave him to die without trying to do something to save him.

I reached down and felt inside his anorak at the bandages. They were still dry, so at least I'd managed to stem the bleeding. What internal bleeding he was suffering I didn't know, but there was nothing to be done about that. If only he would come 'round long enough to answer some questions, it would give me a chance of knowing what best to do.

I drank some beer and ate some chocolate, as the first signs of dawn crept around the mountains.

John Wallace hadn't moved but was still hanging on to life.

My mind made up, I decided I'd return to Zermatt and try to contact the American embassy in Geneva and dump the whole thing in their laps. I would also make an anonymous call to the Swiss air rescue service and tell them there was an injured skier up here. After that I would slip quietly away. It didn't please me to leave with so many loose ends unravelled, but everything was stacked against me, and there seemed little else I could do.

The time for leaving came without a murmur from the injured man, so I packed my haversack including his gun and the money belt. Closing the door firmly I put on my skis and left.

I had climbed two hills, when another thought hit me. If he died before he was rescued, and I was carrying his gun and money belt, I would never be believed. I would then probably spend the rest of my days rotting in prison, or a mental institution.

Somehow the thought didn't bother me too much, as I was just about past caring. Anyway, things couldn't keep going wrong, and by the law of averages I was due for some good luck shortly.

I had just reached the start of my third uphill climb when the sky began releasing its white harvest of smothering flakes. I turned my head upwards, looking into them, and let out a loud sigh. "Whoever you are up there, I wish you'd deal me a fresh hand. I'm bloody fed up with the cards you've given me so far!"

Chapter 7

The journey back to Zermatt was the most strenuous physical endurance test I had ever endured, including that of my army training. I knew how to hang on and force the body through the pain barrier, when willpower alone keeps you going. In competitive games like squash, I had hammered myself unmercifully, just for the satisfaction of winning. Had it not been for this former training and the sheer guts that it builds, I would never have made it. I fell several times in the blizzard, trying to find my way, and it was only the urge for survival that prevented me from giving up. When at last I saw some recognisable ski slopes, I followed them, and some buildings came into view through the storm.

It was a lift station with a restaurant at the bottom, and I staggered in and half collapsed at the nearest table. After I'd eaten and drunk something hot, I continued my journey to Zermatt, following the direction markers. It was after midday when I finally deposited my skis with the hotel porter and took the lift up to my room.

Pouring myself a stiff drink from the room self-service fridge, I sat on the bed and searched the telephone directory for the US embassy. It wasn't listed, so I rang reception and asked the girl if she could get me the number. While I was waiting, I thought that I'd take a bath, as I would hear the phone from the bathroom. After I'd finished bathing, I dressed in some fresh clothes, and after another drink, began to feel almost normal. She still hadn't phoned me back and crossing to the window I saw it had finished snowing and the sky was clearing. Such is the fickleness of mountain weather, I thought. Taking the phone across to the bed, I was about to ring the air rescue service when I noticed the printed number in the centre of the dial.

It was 7.12.73. It was several seconds before it registered on me. 7.12.73 was similar to the number I'd seen on the back of that card. Going to my haversack, I pulled out the money belt and looked at the card. I was right. 7.12.82 was pencilled on the back. It must be a telephone number for him to call, perhaps to contact another agent. The number was so close to the one on my phone, it seemed likely it was another room in this hotel. Many hotels here had direct outside lines installed in each room, and you were charged for the calls when you left. These numbers are listed in the directory and looking it up revealed it was there.

Grand Hotel 7.12.82 was the Grand Hotel room 209.

That meant it was on the next floor. Somehow, I knew this had to be it.

The phone rang, interrupting my thoughts. It was the girl with the embassy number in Geneva.

"Would you like me to ring them for you, sir?" she asked.

"No," I said, "would you connect me with room 209?"

Before she could ring, I had changed my mind.

"No, Miss, I'm sorry, cancel that will you."

"Yes, sir," she said, and I thanked her and hung up.

I thought about it some more and was convinced I was on the right track.

There was only one way to find out, and pocketing the ID card, I went out along the corridor and took the lift to the next floor.

Coming to 209, I knocked and waited. Nothing happened, so I knocked again, louder this time.

More seconds went by and then I heard movement from inside. Finally, the door opened, and she stood there, the surprise on her face matched by the surprise on mine.

Not waiting, I pushed Miss World inside and followed her in, pushing the door shut behind me.

Anger flared in her eyes, as she composed herself, and pulled the dressing gown more tightly around her bare body. She had obviously been under the shower, and her hair was still wrapped in a towel.

"What the hell is this — what do you think you're doing?" she spat out angrily as I pushed her back into the room.

"Don't get excited, precious, I'm not here to rape you," I said quietly, "I believe I have some important information for you."

She hesitated, and relaxing her grip on the dressing

gown, walked around the bed and sat down at the writing table.

"What makes you think you have information that would interest me?" she said, coldly.

She pulled the gown around her knees, but it didn't prevent the top from gaping open, to reveal the beautiful smooth roundness of her breasts.

"This," I said, and producing the ID card. I held it towards her.

Sensing my gaze, she closed the gown to cut off my peep show, as she took the card from me. "What makes you think this concerns me?" she asked, and as she looked at it, I could tell that I'd scored a bullseye.

"Don't let's waste time," I said, confident now that my hunch was right. "This poor bugger's life is in the balance and even now it might be too late."

She stiffened, lowered her hands to her knees and looked up at me anxiously. "What is it you know?"

In her concern she forgot to keep the view covered up, and I could see the slight dampness of her skin, not yet completely dry from the shower. Little beads of water ran down her cleavage, and I could see the firm upward slant of each nipple. They would have won the red sash of honour at Saint- Tropez any day.

My legs felt weak, partly from my previous exertions, and partly from ideas of other exertions that were chasing through my mind as I looked at her.

"Well," she was saying, "what do you know about this man?"

Thinking again about the agent's plight, I felt guilty at my preoccupation. I sat down on the bed and began telling her what had happened. I left out the whereabouts of the hut, and she began asking me how I became involved. I told her enough to convince her, and then she asked for the location of the hut.

"Look," I said, "there's obviously something pretty big going on, for the CIA to have agents chasing about these mountains getting shot up."

I paused for her to say something; when she didn't, I went on. "Well I'll put my cards on the table if you're prepared to do the same."

She looked at me thoughtfully, summing me up, then said, "How can I be sure I can trust you? You come bursting into my room with some way-out story and then expect me to confide in you."

"It's true alright — do you think I'm a bloody looney?" I said angrily.

She rose and walked away, then turned back to me. "If what you say is true, it's very important that I get to this man," then went on, "but in this business there is always the possibility of the other side setting a trap."

I shrugged. "Well the decision's yours," I said. "If you choose to leave that guy up there to die, it'll be on your conscience now and not mine."

She raised her arm and tucked some loose hair back under the towel while she thought about what I'd said.

"Personally," I went on, "If I'm going to get any deeper in this business, there's something I want in return." She was close to me now, and that animal instinct began to occupy my thoughts again.

"What is it you want?" she asked.

It was as much as I could do not to take hold of her and tell her what I'd really like, but I managed to guide my mind back to the situation under discussion.

"Money, I suppose," she went on. "How much do you want?"

"I don't want anything for personal gain," I told her, "but there's something I want taken care of, and I think your people can help. I can't tell you more until I'm sure that you're willing to help me, in return for my helping you."

She went across to the table and my gaze followed the movement of her bare legs as they moved beneath the short robe.

"I have to make a phone call," she said. "What's the number of your room?"

I told her.

"Alright, wait for me there and I'll contact you as soon as I can. Leave me now so that I can get dressed."

I left.

Back in my room I began wondering if I'd done the right thing. Supposing she contacted the authorities and implicated me? It might lead back to the army incident, but it was too late to worry about it now, I just had to wait.

Twenty minutes passed and she hadn't rung, so feeling frustrated, I went back to her room.

There was no answer to my knock, so I hurried down to the lounge to look for her. Checking the dining room, I asked the head waiter if he'd seen her and he replied that he thought he'd seen her go out.

"Damn!" I said.

I was pondering on what to do next, when I glimpsed her passing through the lobby going towards the stairs. I hurried after her and met her as she was about to enter the lift.

"Come up to my room," she said, "there's something we must discuss."

Inside her room, she took off her coat and sat down, beckoning me to do likewise.

"It's a deal," she began, "we're willing to help you, but in return you must tell me exactly where you left our man."

"Fair enough," I said, feeling relieved, "but I still want to know what this is all about, I won't be kept in the dark."

"Alright, I'll level with you," she answered, leaning forwards and locking her fingers around her knees. "It's been left to my judgement to decide if you can be trusted, and I think you can, but we have to move fast."

"You don't need to tell me, I left him there — remember?"

She nodded and went on. "As soon as arrangements are made, they will phone me here with my instructions. Until then there's nothing we can do but wait."

I thought of something we could do, but I didn't

pursue it.

"Suits me," I said, nodding agreement."

"You know already that the CIA are involved here," she continued, "and judging by your concern for our man, I figure that you're morally on our side."

"Go on." I nodded.

"Well this operation also concerns the KGB as well as us, and if I'm wrong about you, my life's not worth a nickel from here on in."

She looked at me intently as she spoke, and I met her gaze as I replied. "You needn't worry, I'm not with the Russians. I don't agree with the way that the US manipulates international politics for their own ends, but the others do the same, and I've no time for communism."

She relaxed. "Good and now that's established, I'll tell you what I know about this."

She leaned back and crossed her legs. "What do you think is the world's biggest problem, and the one that in the long term will have the greatest political consequences?" she asked.

I thought then said, "Well there's oil I guess, and energy in general, but I reckon the spread of nuclear weapons will be number one."

"Wrong, that's number two," she said, "the greatest problem that will soon be facing the world, and the one that will cause the most political strife globally, is the rapidly increasing world's population. The effect of this will make unlimited demands on our ability to produce enough food. We can't go on using fertilisers and other methods that increase yields, it'll cause too much damage to the environment, and even this won't in the end, provide the amount of food that will be needed.

"You've got a point." I agreed. "I've been preaching the same doom and gloom for years. We're on the slippery slope unless something is done to check the population explosion, but with political and religious factions being what they are, I can't see it happening."

"Supposing," she went on, "a way had been found to produce more food, without the use of these methods, but by speeding up and increasing growth and yields. It will double yields without resorting to more chemicals, or other polluting methods, which throw up problems."

"Well," I said, "that sounds fine, but it's only treating the symptom and not the disease. The real answer is to control populations."

"Well maybe," she said, standing up and walking past me to a bottle of drink in the cabinet, "but as you've just said, there's no likelihood of that."

She poured two drinks from the bottle of Gamay, handed one to me, then continued.

"A genetic scientist has discovered a way to modify seeds to speed up growth. This means that yields would double. What's more these plants draw their nutrition from the atmosphere, converting energy from the sun and air; this accelerates their natural growth. It must be rather like the effect you see when a speeded-up film of plant life is played back. I don't know exactly how it's done, but this scientist has proven the results."

As she finished talking, she took a drink, and then put her glass down on the table.

My eyes followed the rhythmic movement of her body, and as I emptied my glass, I went over to the bottle. "May I?" I asked.

"Sure, help yourself," she replied.

I did. "Go on," I said.

"Well the secret is known only to one man. He's an East German scientist, and he's been working in Africa on some lake, where weeds are choking the water by growing rapidly to gigantic sizes. They've spread over hundreds of square miles, and this man was working on a way to control them when he stumbled on the idea of crossing the genus with other plants like wheat and corn. Now after years of research, he's successfully produced a type of plant that provides cereals by this method. He believes he can do the same for a whole range of different foodstuffs. Can you image what this means? And furthermore, he's here in Switzerland!"

I pursed my lips, letting out a low whistle.

"This is dynamite alright, and I can see why the KGB are interested," I said, then went on, pointing my finger to the mountains. "But how does this tie in with your man up there?"

"I'll explain," she said. "This scientist wrote to a colleague in the States telling him of this discovery, and this was passed on to the CIA headquarters in

Washington. They immediately sent out an agent to make contact, and then try to persuade the scientist to go to the States. Unfortunately, the plan was leaked to the Russians, and the KGB got to him first. Professor Linstead — that's his name — panicked and fled to Switzerland, where he asked for political asylum. The Swiss recognised the importance of his work and installed him in a large pharmaceutical laboratory in Geneva."

I was intrigued with her story and waited for her to continue while she finished her drink.

"How come the action's here in Zermatt, if Professor Linstead is in Geneva?" I asked.

She walked across to the bottle and refilled both our glasses.

"He's got a daughter who came with him," she said, handing me my glass, "she's in her teens and is being educated at a private school near Geneva. Several days ago, she came to stay with some school friends in a chalet here in Zermatt for a skiing holiday. Then she was reported missing and we believe the KGB are using her as a hostage, to persuade her father to accept a post in Russia and continue his work there."

"Makes sense," I said, taking a drink.

She went on, "The wounded man you left in the hut is our agent who was working on the kidnap."

"Jesus!" I exclaimed, "They must have mistaken me for your man. No wonder they put me through it, they were trying to find out how close you were getting to them."

She looked at me quizzically. "Now it's your turn to do some explaining," she said.

"Alright," I replied, and gave her the whole story, including the incident at the army post. I felt bad as I thought about the soldier, but it somehow seemed a long time ago, and much had happened since then.

"I expect you've already heard about it," I said.

She hesitated for a moment, then said, "Yes, but we didn't figure it could be connected with the kidnapping."

"I want you to find out if he was married or had any relatives who are in need of help, and I need your people to explain to the Swiss authorities that it was an unfortunate accident," I told her.

"If we agree to that will you help me?" she asked.

"Yes," I answered, "you help the soldier's family, and clear me of any charges, and you can count on me." She bent and took hold of my arm, the faint aroma of her perfume drifting down to me.

"Thanks," she said softly. "You're help will be appreciated — especially by me. And I promise you we'll take care of everything so you've no need to worry about it."

Our eyes met and we held each other's gaze. She was smiling and I was about to reach up and pull her closer when the phone rang and interrupted the mood.

As she turned away to answer it, I was left wondering why she could be so positive about her side of our bargain. Maybe she was conning me, but I could swear that her response was sincere.

The phone call lasted some time and she didn't say much, just the occasional yes and no. Finally, she said, "Alright — yes — I understand," and replaced the receiver.

Turning back to me, she was visibly tenser in her movements. "You must take me to the hut, but first I have to collect some medical supplies and my equipment, then we're to leave at once."

"You don't mean just the two of us?" I queried.

"That's exactly what I mean," she replied.

"But it's one hell of a bloody trip, and what will just the two of us do when we get there?" I asked. Before she could answer, I continued, "Granted you might be able to fix up his wound if we're in time, but what then? He'll not be able to ski, he's too badly hurt."

Moving around to the wardrobe, she began sorting through her clothes before she replied.

"If we get there in time you are to stay with him. Then I must contact another agent in Italy, who will arrange for a rescue team from the Italian side to get him back down to hospital."

I didn't like the idea and didn't think she realised just what she was taking on.

"Look," I said, "I don't like the sound of this, I—" she cut me off before I could finish.

"That's how it is," she cut in, "now quit wasting time and let's get going."

I looked at my watch. "You'll be bloody lucky," I

said getting up, "by the time you've got your gear together we'll have missed the afternoon train up to Gornergrat."

"Isn't there a later one?"

"Well, there's a workman's train that goes as far as Riffelberg, but from there it would be one hell of a climb to the top."

She bit her lip, thinking. "Isn't there any other way up there?"

"What about the Swiss air rescue service?" I suggested. "Couldn't your people arrange for them to take us up by helicopter?"

"No way!" she retorted. "My strict instructions are that we operate alone without involving the Swiss authorities."

"But if you're trying to get the professor's daughter back, surely the Swiss will co-operate, at least on this side of the border. I can't see why we can't—"

"Look," she interrupted again, "you've agreed to help me, and it's got to be done according to my instructions. We are to operate entirely without official help — is that clear?"

"Has anyone ever told you that you look beautiful when you're angry?" I asked.

She softened, "I'm sorry," she said, lowering her eyes, "I guess I'm a little edgy, but I can't afford to screw this up, please understand that."

The appeal in her voice awakened my Sir Galahad instinct, and a thought struck me.

"There could be another way," I said quickly.

"There's a private chopper service that I've used before, and it's possible it could get us to the hut before nightfall, if I can persuade them to take us up."

Her face lit up and she smiled.

"That's great — you get off and arrange it while I pick up the gear. Where is it?"

"It's a heliport near the station," I said, heading for the door, "but I can't promise they'll do it."

She caught my hand as I opened the door, and for a moment we stood together in the doorway. Her perfume came across much stronger this time. She pressed herself against me, then lifted her head and brushed her lips lightly across mine.

"You can fix it," she whispered, "I know you can," and, squeezing my hand, said, "by the way my name's Kim Summers."

"Pleased to meet you, Kim," I replied, "mine's Sands — Matt Sands."

She released my hand.

"I'll meet you there in twenty minutes, Matt," she said, and closed the door.

Back in my room the sensation of that brief kiss still lingered, as I collected my things together for the journey. Pocketing the American's money, as well as my own, I considered which gun to take and decided on mine, leaving his in the wardrobe. Checking that I had everything, I put on my anorak and left.

Going down in the lift, I was excited by the thought of the action about to come, but the thoughts of that doorway embrace persisted still.

Chapter 8

The office at the heliport was about to close as I got there, but the girl who was just leaving let me in. I thanked her and closed the door behind her as she left. There was a young man in the office also preparing to leave.

"I'm afraid we're just closing, sir," he said politely in English, realising my nationality. "What is it you require?"

"I want to charter a helicopter to take me and a friend up to Stockhorn above Gornergrat," I said.

"That will be perfectly possible," he replied. "When did you want to go?"

"Now," I said.

He looked surprised.

"Oh, but I'm afraid that's not possible, sir, you see we have stopped operating for today. Also, by the time you got there it would be rather late to ski back again before dark."

"We're not skiing back here," I told him. "We're skiing down to a night stop on the Italian side, and then commencing a tour tomorrow morning."

He looked at me disapprovingly.

"Well, sir, I don't wish to criticise, but here in

Zermatt we try to discourage unaccompanied ski touring — it's very dangerous when you are unfamiliar with these mountains."

"Yes, I know about that, but I've done this before and I'm very experienced, you've no need to worry about our safety," I assured him. His face showed his uncertainty as he pondered on my request, and without waiting I went on,

"Look, find a pilot to get us up there, and if he considers that the conditions are dangerous when we land, I'll agree to him bringing us back here," I lied.

"The pilot's no problem," he said, looking out of the window, "I do the piloting for the ski tours, as I know these mountains."

"Then you know it's okay right now," I bullshitted him, "the snow is just great and we've got time to get there in daylight."

Fishing in my pocket, I brought out the folded five hundred-franc notes that I'd taken from the money belt. Peeling off two, I held them towards him. "This will cover it," I said, "and you can take your girlfriend out to dinner with the rest." It wasn't my money, and it wouldn't do the American any good if we didn't get to him soon.

The pilot hesitated and I knew he was hooked. Not waiting, I pushed it into his hand. He walked over to the telephone.

"One moment," he said.

Speaking in Swiss Deutsch, he had a rapid

conversation with someone, then called over to me. "If you can be ready in ten minutes, I will take you up."

Nodding my approval, I turned as a noise came from outside, and seconds later the door opened, and Kim came in.

"Is everything alright, Matt?" she asked.

"Yes, it's all fixed, we'll be taking off in a few minutes, they're getting the chopper ready now."

"Good," she said, "I've got the medic pack."

The pilot had disappeared into another room and reappeared wearing his flying rig. As he spotted Kim, I told him, "This is my friend, Miss Summers."

Smiling, he stepped forward and shook her outstretched hand.

"I'm not exactly in favour of your going up, Miss Summers, and had I known the other passenger was a woman, I might not have agreed."

Like bloody hell you wouldn't, I thought, what, for a thousand francs!

"Don't worry about me, I've plenty of experience," Kim told him, "just treat me like another man."

"I'm sure I'll find that very difficult," he said, turning on his come-hither smile.

Saucy bastard, I thought, now he's trying his luck. Oh well all's fair I suppose.

"It will be necessary to warm up the helicopter before we take off," he told us. "Keep a look-out and I'll signal to you when I'm ready."

He left us watching through the window, and when

he signalled to us, we hurried out towards the helicopter.

"You take the haversacks and I'll bring the skis. Did you get some climbing skins?" I asked.

"Yes, they're in the rucksack," Kim replied.

We ran across the flattened snow and bundled in with our equipment. Minutes later we were airborne above the village.

The helicopter followed the railway as far as Riffelalp, swung across to Findela and then up to the lower part of the glacier. Flying over the northern slopes below Triftji, we continued to gain height until the restaurant at Rote Nase came into view. Skirting the north face of the Monte Rosa, we flew on in its shadow towards the summit of Stockhorn.

Indicating to the pilot where I wanted him to land, he circled a couple of times before putting down.

Not giving him a chance to argue, I threw out our equipment, and pushing Kim out onto the fixed ladder, I followed her down and dropped off into the snow.

Dragging the packs clear we waved goodbye, and seconds later the chopper, with its orange light flashing, was disappearing into the evening sky.

As the cold closed in around us, we struggled into the pack harness and stepped into our skis.

"That guy had a point when he questioned bringing us up here," I said.

Kim finished fixing the skins.

"Well, we're here now, and the sooner we get to the hut the better," she answered, then added, "I hope you can still find the way."

The same thought had crossed my mind, but I didn't let on.

"You follow me as close as you can, and I'll try and make it as easy as possible for you, by traversing where it's possible. If you get into difficulty, shout like crazy and I'll stop," I told her.

Kim looked at me and laughed.

"Don't twist your balls worrying about me, ski-man," she said. "I won the interstate downhill two years running, before I left college."

I laughed back.

"Well life's full of surprises," I joked. "I'll try not to slow you up, but I like to explore the angles where it's soft and the turns are wide and easy."

She tested her weight against her heel releases, then gave me an impish grin as the double meaning of my remark got through to her.

"I'll remember that, Matt." She giggled.

Finding the hut proved easier than I had expected. The approach route was familiar, but my legs were getting tired after the day's exertions. Kim hadn't exaggerated about her ability, and wherever I skied she was right behind me. I didn't doubt that had she known the way; she would have left me standing. I stopped above the hut and she slewed to a perfect parallel stop beside me.

I lifted my ski stick and pointed down.

"That's it," I said quietly."

We stood looking down in the fading light. Not a sound came from anywhere, except for the faint murmur of the late afternoon wind.

I turned to speak to her and began,

"I hope we're not too late and you know how to patch up his bullet wounds when we—" but she wasn't listening, and before I could finish the sentence her ski trails were already sending up plumes of loose snow as she made the descent.

Following her down, I stopped some distance from the door, where she was already unfastening her skis in readiness to go in. I approached cautiously, taking out my pistol in case of trouble. By the time I reached the door and released my skis, she was already inside. Gripping the gun in case something was wrong, I hesitated a moment before going in. The light was fading now, making it difficult to see inside. As I stepped forward, Kim met me at the doorway. Her goggles were pushed up onto her hat, and her face was pale and without its former humour.

"He's dead," she said, grabbing my outstretched arm.

Leaving her at the entrance, I went past her into the hut. The semi-darkness in the hut made proper vision difficult, but I could see him bundled up against the far side. Pocketing the pistol, I dumped my pack and fished out the torch for a closer look. By its light I could see the body of the CIA man, rolled over on its side against the wall. I bent and rolled him over so that his head came around to face me, and almost threw up at the sight. I had never seen a man with his brains blown out.

Forcing myself to look, I saw that one side of his skull was completely shattered, leaving a gaping hole between where his left eye and ear should have been. Congealed blood covered the mangled pulp and bone that hung down onto his shoulder.

John Wallace hadn't died from his previous wound. Someone had shot him from close range with what must have been a heavy calibre weapon, to have caused so much damage.

Letting the body rest back against the wall, I straightened up.

"I hope that you never regained consciousness before this happened to you, old son," I said quietly and went back outside.

Kim was leaning against the outside wall, and there was enough light for me to see the tears that were running down her cheeks.

I spoke quietly to her.

"There's nothing we can do here now, Kim, we'd better make it down on this side and find a place for the night before the light goes completely."

She brushed her cheek with the sleeve of her anorak.

"We must get rid of the body first — then we'll go down." Her voice was strained as she spoke, and I could see she was fighting to control her feelings.

"Look," I objected, "this bloke's been murdered, we just can't dump his body. You'll have to report it to your people, and they'll have to sort it out with the Swiss and Italian police."

She turned angrily towards me as she spoke.

"No! My instructions were clear. If we got here too late, I was to get rid of any evidence of our man's presence, then carry on and meet another of our agents who is on his way from Milan."

I continued to argue but it was no use.

"If you haven't the guts to help me, I'll do it alone," she said, almost hysterically, "but we made a deal, and I thought you were the kind of guy to see a thing through once you'd started."

Put like that I could hardly refuse, and I couldn't let her struggle on her own with the gruesome mess inside the hut. In any case I was deeply involved now and dumping a dead body wouldn't make much difference.

"Let's get on with it," I said grimly.

Kim held the torch while I pulled the remains of the sleeping bag over the top of the corpse and tied it down under the shoulders. Taking the body by its feet I dragged it across the floor and out into the snow. There was just enough light for us to spot a deep gully nearby. It took us both all our strength to drag the dead body across to the edge and push it over to a snowy grave among the rocks below.

It was a pretty gruesome business, but not once did she falter. Her emotions had shown through a moment ago, but now she had an iron grip on herself.

We walked back to the hut without speaking, then

selecting our route down, we collected our gear and skied off.

Kim went ahead, and as we reached the tree line the light was so bad, I had to stop at times, sometimes only managing to sidestep between the snowdrifts. I swore as I fell several times but was able to scramble up and carry on. Coming out of the forest, the light was better, and I could see her standing below me on the edge of a clearing. The early night sky was still bright here, as it often is before darkness falls. Below to the left, and again further south, the twinkling lights of several villages glimmered in the otherwise darkened valley.

Kim was leaning forwards on her sticks when I reached her.

"Where do you reckon we are?" she asked.

"As near as I can tell we must be looking down on two Italian villages — they could be Pecetto and Macugnaga." I said.

She nodded.

"Then we best make for the largest one and find a place for the night. I must phone in and report as soon as I can."

"Suits me," I replied.

With that she was off again, but slower this time, and I found it easier to follow her path.

We were soon on level ground and trudging along towards the largest village about a mile ahead. Guided by its lights, we were soon onto a hard road and continued the rest of the journey on foot, carrying our skis. The night air was surprisingly warm in the sheltered valley, and although still below freezing, felt much less cold, after coming from the sub-zero temperatures of the higher altitudes.

The village was a scattered collection of streets, and the dim lights showed a tatty looking hotel sign, on the wall of a large crumbling building on the outskirts. Further on we passed a couple of pension houses that were equally dim and tatty. Not a soul came into sight as we plodded along. In the centre of the village the buildings took on a more respectable appearance. Opposite a 'Funivia' station was a reasonable looking hotel. It was the 'Alberto Blanco' and as we approached, Kim caught my arm and held me back.

"Do you speak Italian?" she asked in a low voice.

"Two words," I replied.

"Then let me do the talking and keep quiet. We shouldn't create too much attention as skiers, but Americans and English will be rare around here, and we can't take any chances."

I nodded, "You're not kidding," I said and followed her up the steps to the entrance.

Inside the large hall, a reception desk at the far end was lit by a solitary electric light bulb that hung from the ceiling. Dark panelled stairs led up each side and an elderly woman in black sat at the desk. On the wall behind her were wooden pigeon-holes, most of which had keys hanging on the hooks below them. She didn't bother to look up as we entered and dumped our skis but continued writing in a large ledger on the desk in front of her.

Kim spoke to the old woman in Italian, and she lifted her head and squinted at us. By the conversation that followed there seemed to be some difficulty in arranging our accommodation.

Producing a passport, Kim continued to argue, until the old woman gave in and hunted along the pigeon-holes for a key. Taking it from her, Kim pushed some folded notes across the desk and said something in a low voice. The old crab picked up the money and chuckling to herself, came out and led the way up one of the flights of stairs.

The room she showed us was huge and surprisingly well furnished. In the middle was the largest bed I'd ever seen, measuring at least eight feet across, and high enough off the floor for a squadron of cavaliers to have hidden beneath it. The French windows, I felt sure, must lead out onto a creeper covered balcony.

Saying something to Kim, the old woman winked, then scurried off muttering and chuckling to herself as she disappeared through the door.

Dumping my pack on the floor, I sank into the spacious armchair by the bed.

"What was that all about?" I asked.

Kim smiled wanly.

"I told the old crow we were ski touring and wanted a meal and a room for the night. She wanted us to leave our passports, but I said you were a German businessman, and your passport was back in your car where we were heading. Before she got too inquisitive, I gave her enough lira to shut her up, and I think she takes us for a couple of pleasure seekers needing a place for a night's screwing."

Smiling back at her, I couldn't resist a joke. "Judging by the size of that bed, I'd exhaust myself trying to pin you down." I laughed.

Her face relaxed and some of its former softness returned. Kim leaned against the bed and looked at me.

"It's been a long, hard day, Matt," she said, "and it's not over yet. By the time we get to bed tonight both of us will only be fit for sleeping."

"Can I take a rain check?" I asked, only half joking. She smiled but said nothing. Leaning there she looked almost like a child, and I realised that she had a lot of guts to have come through these last few hours. Reaching up from the armchair, I took her hand and held it while I spoke.

"What passport do you have that didn't give the game away that you're an American — and where did you learn the lingo like that?"

"They gave me a Swiss passport for cover, and I collected a wad of lira and the medical stuff before I met you at the heliport; the Italian comes from my grandmother. She was Italian."

I released her hand. "You must have a good organisation in Switzerland," I said.

"We have — I wish it was as good on this side of

123

the border." She walked across to the French windows and stood looking out for a few moments, then closed the curtains and came back to me.

"I have to go out and make a phone call," she said. "I can't do it from here as I don't trust that old woman downstairs. I must get through to our people and let them know we're here and arrange for our man in Milan to meet us."

"Shall I come with you?" I asked.

"No, Matt, it's best you stay here, this place could be crawling with KGB agents and commie sympathisers and you might be recognised. We can't be far away from where they held you captive, when they mistook you for John Wallace."

"Yes, I've been thinking about that," I said, standing up and stretching my back.

"By my reckoning that mountain chalet must be just north of here, between Monte Rosa and the Monte Moro Pass. They're using a helicopter, and that's probably how they caught up with John Wallace and finished him off. They left him dead but know that I'm still alive and they'll be hunting for me, as they think I'm a danger to them."

Kim's face tensed again.

"Right," she said, "I think my cover's okay. But you must be careful, Matt, if they catch up with you, you'll finish up like John." She seemed on the verge of crying but managed to hold back.

"Did you know him well?" I asked softly.

"No, not really. I only met him three or four times, but he was very kind to me when I needed it."

"Why don't you tell me about it?"

She crossed to the door.

"Not now, Matt, I must get that call through. Lock the door after me and keep your gun handy. I shouldn't be long, but don't take any unnecessary chances while I'm away."

"Don't worry," I said, "my body might be pooped but my mind's still clicking, and I've no intention of letting anyone finish me off yet."

She nodded approval and left.

I locked the door, took my pistol and turned off the lights. Going to the curtains, I stood looking out. I could see through the balcony rails to the building opposite, and the dimly lit street below. Kim left our hotel, and crossing the street, made off along the slushy road towards the brighter lights of the village centre. I watched her go out of sight then went back and sat down.

It was almost unbelievable. To think that only a few days ago I was enjoying a peaceful skiing holiday. Now, here I was in the middle of an international intrigue between the two largest intelligence networks in the world, involving kidnap and murder. I was feeling whacked right now, but that would be okay by morning, after a good night's sleep.

Mentally I was wound up, and sitting thinking about it, I realised that I was enjoying the stimulus of the excitement and danger. The soldier's death gave me regret, sure, but we are what we are, and I couldn't help feeling excited about the whole business.

I couldn't be sure that I'd get my revenge for all that had happened, but I'd sure as hell try. There must be a way up to that chalet from this side and if this was the nearest village they would probably come here for supplies.

I got up and went back to the window. Nothing had changed, and I could see it was a clear night and the temperature would be dropping fast. A few people were beginning to get about, and the slush was already crunching beneath their feet. After another ten minutes or so I recognised Kim coming back to the hotel. Walking briskly, she soon disappeared beneath the balcony on her way to the hotel entrance. I continued watching for a minute or two, in case she was being followed. I didn't think that she could be, but like she'd said, when your life is the price you pay for your first mistake, one is one too many. Satisfied that no one had followed her, I crossed to the door and waited.

There was a gentle tap,

"Matt, it's me, Kim."

Unlocking the door, I opened it and let her in.

"Leave the lights off till I draw the curtains," I said, as she closed the door behind her. "Okay, now you can switch them on."

The room lit up and she pulled off her anorak and threw it over a chair.

"I'll make a field man of you yet," she grinned, "but

put that gun away, or you'll scare the pants off whoever brings us our meal. I've arranged with the old witch downstairs to send it up to our room. She's agreed, but I had to sweeten her with some more lira."

I put the pistol in my anorak.

"Did you get through okay?" I asked.

"Yes, the professor's daughter's been taken, and he's already been contacted. He's making arrangements to leave, and the Swiss are powerless to stop him. Unless we can grab back the girl, he'll be en route to Russia, via a satellite country." She sighed before going on.

"That will put in their hands the biggest bargaining weapon imaginable, on the underdeveloped countries needing to solve their food problems. That will leave the US losing their influence over these countries. Can you begin to imagine what that means?"

I nodded.

"Do your people know where the girl is being held?"

"No, but it's likely to be near here, for John was pretty close to them. It could be the same place you were taken, and we must ski the area and hope to find the chalet where you were held."

I thought for a moment before I answered.

"The trouble is, I'd come up from the Swiss side when they intercepted me at the hut, and I've no idea of the area on this side of the border."

"I know," she replied, "but there can't be many remote chalets with a plateau big enough to land a helicopter around here, and the locals might be able to give us some clues tomorrow."

The idea of asking around didn't appeal to me at all.

"If we go asking around for that sort of information, it will give us away for sure," I said.

"I know, Matt, but we'll have to gamble on finding them before they're tipped off and come after us."

"I thought you said not to take chances?" I challenged her.

Kim raised her eyebrows as she spoke. "I said not to take unnecessary chances, this is necessary. We've got no choice if we're to find the girl in time to prevent the professor from leaving."

Remembering her phone call, I asked,

"What about your chap from Milan?"

"He'll be here in the morning to join up with us. He's skied this area often and should be a big help."

There was a knock on the door, and Kim spoke in Italian to someone outside before she opened it. A pimply-faced lad in a white jacket came in pushing a trolley. He greeted me in Italian and exchanged some more conversation with Kim. I nodded and retired to the adjoining bathroom until he'd gone. When I returned, Kim was setting the table with a couple of chairs that the waiter had brought from the corridor. Kim finished arranging the plates and glasses and looking up, said,

"Gee this looks good, I hope you're feeling hungry."

I went to lock the door, but she had already thought of it.

"Hungry and thirsty," I said, noticing the bottle of Chianti."

We settled down together and helped ourselves from the trolley. There was a huge pizza, a plate of cold meats, a mixed vegetable salad and the wine. On the shelf beneath was a large bowl of fruit and a cheese board.

We spoke little during the meal, but towards the end the Chianti had relaxed us, and we began talking again. Kim had turned off the main light before we ate, and we sat eating by the glow from the wall light over the bed. The effect of the wine, plus the warmth from the old iron radiators, which belied the freezing conditions outside, had made it necessary for us to strip down to just ski pants and shirts.

I looked across at her.

"How did a beautiful girl like you get mixed up in a business like this?" I asked, scoring myself nil out of ten for the originality of the question.

She leaned forwards towards me with her elbows on the table and rested her chin on her knuckles. "Through my husband," she said.

I'd somehow not thought of her being married, and I waited in silence for her to continue.

After a moment, she went on,

"I was working for the treasury department when we met, and a month later we were married. It was one of those things where two people think they are made for each other." I sipped some wine and she went on.

"Bill was with the CIA, though I didn't know it at the time. Before we were married, he told me his work with the government was secret and could be dangerous. We honeymooned in South America, and as we were leaving for the return flight, Bill got a call at the airport. He told me that I would have to fly back home alone, and he would join me later. Something had come up, and he would have to deal with it before he could return." She took a drink then said, "I never saw him again — his body was eventually recovered from an old mineshaft." She opened her fingers, letting her head drop into her hands, covering her eyes.

Reaching forwards across the table, I took hold of her wrists.

"I'm sorry, Kim," I murmured. "I know that's the standard answer, and I wish there was something else I could say that was more helpful, but there isn't anything."

Lifting her head, she blinked away the tears and smiled at me.

"It's alright," she said, "it was four years ago. You'd think I'd be over it by now but sometimes it all comes back to me."

"If it still hurts don't let's talk about it, I know how you must be feeling."

"No, Matt, I'd like to tell you about it."

We drank the last of the wine and held hands across the table.

"Shortly after Bill's death, I heard that he'd been

killed by the KGB while trying to contact one of their agents, who wanted to defect to the West. I was shattered and couldn't work or face my friends. That was when John Wallace came to see me. He persuaded me to go back to my job in the treasury, and I gradually got my life together again. I met John a couple of times after that, and by then I'd decided that I'd like to do some active work with the CIA if it could be arranged. I asked him about it, and at first he tried to talk me out of it, but when he saw I was determined, he made the necessary arrangements for me to be enrolled."

"Did you work with him then?" I asked.

"No. You see John wasn't an agent in the strictest sense of the word. He was really a security man, and in fact was over here in Rome advising on the security arrangements for the Pope's visit to America, when this business with the professor blew up."

"Then what was he doing here?" I queried.

"He was sent up to liaise with our Swiss group to help sort this out. That's how he was carrying identification when you found him and patched him up."

"I see," I said.

Kim looked at her watch.

"What say we push this lot out into the corridor and get some sleep."

I rose and loaded the dishes onto the trolley.

"I sure won't need any rocking," I said.

Unlocking the door to push out the trolley, the pimply waiter was standing there. He said something, but I merely ignored it and pushed the trolley at him. He hesitated for a moment then turned and made off with the trolley. Closing and locking the door I wondered how long he'd been outside.

Turning back into the room, the thought was still troubling me when Kim came through from the bathroom. She was only wearing her undies, and I lost all thoughts of the waiter. Climbing into bed and pushing back the covers, she sat for a moment with her legs drawn up in readiness to slide down under the sheets.

"Which side do you like, Matt?" she asked, the smallness of her waist emphasising the feminine roundness of her hips as she sat there.

"At any other time, the same side as you," I answered, grinning at her, "but tonight I'll take the east flank nearest the door."

She slid under the bedclothes and looked up at me, her tousled hair on the pillow, and one arm crooked over her head.

"You're okay, Matt," she said, "it's great having you on the team — thanks again."

Once again, her beauty stirred things deep inside me, with a chemistry that I could feel interacting between us.

I smiled down at her.

"Any time," I said, and switching off the light, I undressed and got into bed.

Chapter 9

The night passed without incident. The effort of the past days coupled with the meal and wine had knocked me out so completely an earthquake wouldn't have disturbed me. I came out of my sleep with Kim rousing me. She was already dressed in her skiing gear.

I sat up and stretched, pleased that my previous stiffness had gone. The room was filled with pale sunlight that was shafting through the French windows. One of them was open, and the crisp freshness of the air entering the bedroom brought me out of my sleepiness.

"I've brought you some breakfast," Kim said. "How do you like your morning coffee?"

Leaning back against the thick bolster, I drew in a couple of deep breaths, enjoying the fresh air.

"No sugar, but I can't stand the strong stuff they have out here, so weaken it down with plenty of milk."

She brought it over and handed it to me. "There's no milk, only cream and not much of that."

I took the cup and tasted a sip.

"Bloody bitter old muck," I complained. "What do they make it with, goat shit?"

She laughed and brought me over a pastry. "Here, have one of these to take away the taste — they're pretty good."

"Thanks."

The crumbs from it stuck to my lips and fell off onto the sheets. Noticing my predicament, Kim took the cup and handed me a serviette.

"You keep yourself in good shape," she said, placing her hand on my bare shoulder.

"You haven't seen the half of it," I said, grinning, spraying out little bits of the flaky pastry as I spoke. "Care for a conducted tour?"

She put her hand to her mouth in mock horror and stood back, laughing.

"Wipe your mouth," she giggled, "you look like some darn kid who found the cookies."

I laughed and asked her the time.

"It's ten after nine, and you'd better be shaking your arse out of there, we've got work to do."

Walking to the end of the bed, Kim stood looking down at me, and then without warning, she grabbed the bed covers and jerked them off onto the floor.

"Hey!" I yelled, trying to hang on to the top sheet. But I was too late, and I was left uncovered except for my jockey pants.

Rolling off the bed, I made around towards her. The cold air from the open window hit me full blast, causing armies of goose pimples to rise up all over me. Kim was holding the bedclothes in front of her and giggling.

"Right," I said in mock anger, "you've asked for it!"

Launching myself at her, we both fell in a tangled

heap of blankets and bed linen, rolling about in fake battle. She was much stronger than her femininity indicated and had obviously been trained to take care of herself. Before I could prevent her, she half dragged off my pants and I felt her teeth marks on the top of my buttocks. Squirming around on the floor in fits of laughter, she finally succumbed to my fifty pounds weight advantage. I pinned her beneath me and lay across her chest, holding down her arms above her head.

We both looked at each other and suddenly stopped laughing.

Lowering my head, I kissed her nose, and felt her body soften. Releasing her arms, I slid one hand beneath her shoulders, and with the other, pushed away the heap of blankets, as I moved across on top of her. As I fumbled to undo her ski pants, she stopped me and put her hand against my chest, holding me off.

"No, Matt," she whispered, "please."

I hesitated, then eased off.

She went on,

"We've had a laugh and now it's time to go to work — there'll be another time."

"Promise?" I asked.

"Promise."

I moved back as we looked at each other momentarily. Then, conscious of the cold air from the window, I got up and picked up the pile of crumpled bed clothes.

"You'd better shower and get dressed now, Matt,

our guy from Milan will be here shortly."

Turning into the bathroom, I looked back at her as she rearranged the bed.

"That's worked off my aches and pains." I laughed, then dropped my gaze. "But I'm still rather stiff, don't you think?" I said.

Kim looked at my naked profile.

"You should take a cold shower," she called mockingly, throwing a pillow at me as I closed the bathroom door.

Taking her advice, I let the cold water run all over me as it rinsed off the soap. I turned the shower off and towelled off vigorously, and then heard voices from the bedroom. They were speaking in Italian, and I thought it was the waiter collecting the breakfast things.

I dressed and went out. Kim was standing by the window talking to a rather thin, dapper, little man probably in his thirties. Dark hair cut short and inclined to curl was receding noticeably from his rather high forehead. He had a thin moustache and sharp features that were dominated by his large brown eyes.

Kim introduced him.

"This is Renato Sergia."

We shook hands.

"Matt Sands," I said.

He smiled pleasantly and spoke to me in English. "Pleased to meet you, Mr Sands, I understand that you are new to this business."

"That's right," I replied, "and I'm beginning to

think there are easier ways of reaching retirement."

"There is always the danger of course," he said, then looking across at the bed, "but the job has certain other compensations."

Looking first at Kim, then back at Renato, I replied.

"Well, all I've got so far is a recommendation for a good conduct medal."

He shook his head and grinned, then the three of us began to discuss our plan of action.

Renato said he would drive along to the next village and try to find out if any helicopters were operating in this area. He turned to me.

"If you and Kim take the chairlift from here, you can ski the area and try to spot the chalet," he said.

I nodded and Kim agreed.

"We'll meet back here at lunch time," she replied, as we prepared to leave.

The weather didn't fulfil its earlier promise, and a lot of cloud closed in around the mountains. We were unable to spot anything that looked like the chalet, although we did see a helicopter away to the west. Hoping that Renato had been luckier than us, we returned to the hotel.

Renato was already there waiting for us.

"We're in luck," he began excitedly, "there's a helicopter service along in the next village. It's run by two brothers, and it's the only one in this area. They take skiers up to high altitude tours when conditions are favourable."

I looked at Kim.

"Could be it," I said.

Before she could reply, Renato cut in,

"There's something more. They often fly up and back, even if there are no skiers, because they own a chalet in the mountains."

"That's got to be it." I said, "What do you think, Kim?"

She turned to me and started to say something, then changed her mind and turned back to Renato.

"Has anyone seen them with a girl?" she asked him.

"Well no, but I got my information from a waitress, and she was new to the area. All the locals I spoke to were tight lipped, and I didn't want to appear too inquisitive. I think there's something going on, and the two brothers seem to run the village, and no one interferes."

We stood thinking about it and Kim was first to break the silence.

"We've got a problem," she said. "It's pretty damn obvious that we've tracked them down, but what now?" She went on. "We can't just storm the place by force and finding the chalet without being spotted is pretty unlikely, even if we can find it."

Renato was first to answer her.

"Why not hire the helicopter to take us up for a ski tour, and with luck we might spot the chalet. After they drop us off, we could ski back to it, and if the girl's being held there, we could surprise them."

"That's pretty chancy," Kim said, "and if we got away with it, how would we make it back down with the girl once we'd shown our hand?"

"We've only one chance as I see it," I said. "Now they've contacted the professor, and he's preparing to leave, they will have to bring the girl down to join him. He wouldn't consent to work for them without her."

Kim nodded.

"So, what's your plan?" she asked.

"Well." I went on. "They'll have to bring her down by helicopter, and the chances are they'll take her by car from here to meet up with the professor. There's only one road from here down the valley, so we could intercept them further down."

Kim nodded.

"You're right, Matt, and they'll be making their move any moment. Professor Linstead won't agree to leave before he has proof that his daughter is safe and well."

Renato had produced a map and was already studying it as Kim joined him.

"My guess is they'll drive her and the professor to Trieste," Kim said, "then go via Yugoslavia to the Eastern Bloc."

Renato nodded and Kim went on,

"Our problem is knowing where to be at the right time, and knowing the car they'll be in."

I was already thinking about it. We couldn't prepare an ambush without knowing their car, and when they were leaving. Besides that, we only had Renato's car and couldn't be in both places at once.

Kim turned to Renato.

"There's only one thing for it," she said forcefully, "we'll have to stake out the helicopter pad at the village and wait for them to make their move. As soon as we spot them with the girl, we'll try to beat them down the valley and hope for a chance to intercept them."

Renato snapped his fingers.

"Right," he said, "they are bound to make the descent in daylight, and we'll have the chance to see how strong they are."

They both looked at me enquiringly.

"Okay," I said. "It's pretty thin, but right now I can't think of anything better."

Ten minutes later we had left the hotel and were driving to the next village. The sign showed 'Pecetto' as Renato slowed the car and pulled into the car park.

We unloaded our skis and made our way through the village towards the buildings that stood beside the helicopter landing area. The snow fields on either side were being used as nursery slopes. We mingled with the beginners and pretended to practise some basic movements. Half an hour passed, and nothing happened.

Kim faked an uncontrolled turn and fell at my feet, knocking me over with her. Laughing and helping me up, she spoke to me in a low voice.

"Let's work our way down to the buildings, there doesn't seem to be anyone about, and I'd like to get a closer look at the layout."

"Alright, you lead off and I'll follow," I told her.

Seeing our move, Renato disentangled himself from the group of Italians enjoying themselves on the opposite slope and began a jerky descent to join us.

We skirted the flattened snow of the landing pad, keeping to the outside of the plastic rope and coloured poles, each topped with a small red flag to mark the perimeter. Following a path that led through the buildings, we could see into the main hangar as we passed. It was empty except for a small red Fiat that was parked just inside the open door. Coming around to the side window, I caught Kim's arm and pulled her back behind the pillar that divided it.

"In there! Across the far side, by the filing cabinet — it's the girl that was up at the chalet with Garlic Mouth!" I whispered quickly.

Kim looked. "Are you sure, Matt?"

I didn't answer but instead turned and motioned to Renato to stay where he was, but he didn't understand and advanced to join us behind the pillar.

"Matt's recognised the girl inside," Kim told him. "She's one of the gang."

Renato nodded, and bending to undo his skis, he took a casual look through the window as he straightened up. "She appears to be alone," he whispered.

Kim turned to me.

"This is it. The others must still be up at the chalet with

the professor's daughter. Me and Renato will go in and grab her, and then we can surprise them when they come down."

Renato was leaning his skis against the pillar, clipping them together. He could see inside from where he was standing, and dropping one of the clips, he spoke to us as he bent down to recover it.

"I think she's about to leave, she's putting on her coat."

Kim swore, and as she did, I heard the door as the girl made her departure. Quickly stooping, I fumbled with my ski bindings to hide my face, as Kim stepped across between me and the girl.

Merely glancing at us, she locked the door and walked past us to the open hangar. As we waited, we heard the sound of a car door, then the engine fired, and the little red Fiat drove out past us towards the village. Renato had already reached the end of the buildings, and as the Fiat turned out, he quickly followed it on foot, trying to keep it in sight.

"That's screwed my plan," Kim said angrily. "Come on, we'll catch Renato and find somewhere to stay here; it doesn't look as though they intend making their move today."

We shouldered our skis and walked off. We turned into the main street and were half-way along when Renato came hurrying back towards us.

"We're in luck," he panted, his brown eyes wide with excitement. "She turned off in the village onto a track to a farm. It's only a hundred metres away, and she's gone in and left the car parked outside."

"Is there anyone else there?" Kim lowered her skis as she shot the question.

"I couldn't tell, but there's a forest behind, so if we circle from here, we can come up from behind and get close without being spotted."

Kim stepped into her skis and doing likewise, I followed behind her and Renato. Reaching the trees, we carried on and circled back to the farm. It was easy to get close, and we watched for some time without being seen.

The little red car stood on the rutted snow outside, and inside the farmhouse nothing stirred. Signalling for me and Renato to follow, Kim advanced to behind a large snow-covered bush and waited for us to join her.

"This is the plan." she told us. "There are no other vehicles here, so the girl is probably alone in there. It's the ideal spot to make our move so here's what we do." She turned to Renato.

"You and me will go to the door and ask the way to the ski school. When she comes to the door, I'll bundle her inside, and you take care of anyone else who might be there. If it's not the girl who answers the door, stick your gun in their ribs and I'll go in and get the girl. Got that?"

Renato nodded and began examining his gun.

Kim turned to me.

"Matt, once we're inside if things go wrong, be ready to give us cover as we come out."

"Don't worry," I said.

Then reaching out and taking her shoulder, I pulled her close and spoke seriously.

"There could be several of them in there, Kim, wouldn't it be better to continue watching till we're sure?"

She looked at me, her expression showing no sign of faltering.

"No, I have to chance it. She might leave and drive away any minute, and we can't afford to lose her now."

She was right.

Renato was ready to go, and they started for the farm.

"What happens if there's shooting and no one comes out?" I asked.

"Then you're on your own and you'll have to—" The rest of her reply was lost to me, as they gathered speed down the hill.

Watching from my hiding place, I saw them finish the descent and approach the farmhouse.

I took out my gun and fumbled with the safety catch and wondered what range the old pistol had. If it came to a shoot-out, I wouldn't be much help to them if I was out of distance.

Leaving their skis, they approached the door, and my pulse quickened at the thought of the action that was about to happen. Next moment the door opened, and after a short scuffle they were inside, and the door swung shut.

A minute passed, then another and no sound came from inside.

"Christ, what the hell's going on?" I asked myself aloud.

I was about to ski down, when the door opened and the white face of Renato appeared, followed by his slim body, as he cautiously stepped out into full view. Looking up to where he knew I was hiding, he beckoned me to go down. Then without waiting he went back inside, and the door closed.

"I'm not sure I like the look of this," I said, speaking to myself again. "I think I'll do a little investigating of my own."

I put the pistol back on safety and zipped it into my side pocket, then retreated into the wood and skied around to the other side of the farmhouse. There were cowsheds there screening the house, and crossing to them I kicked off my skis, and ran knee deep through the snow to the rear corner of the house. Unzipping the gun, I prepared it for action, then ducked and ran the rest of the distance to bring me to the side of the rear window. Everything remained quiet, and stooping to keep below the window, I slowly edged around the old shutter that was fixed open against the wall, and gradually raised my head to look in.

It was the kitchen, and there was no one inside. I crept away, passing beneath the closed shutters of the upstairs windows and came to the front corner. Then I heard the door open as someone came out. Next instant the figure of a man appeared around the corner towards me, almost bumping into my outstretched gun.

In frightened amazement, he flung himself sideways into the snow.

"Don't shoot!" he cried, gazing up with his brown eyes bolting, showing both fear and relief at the same time.

I lowered the gun, laughing and stepped forwards to help him up. If anything, Renato's face was even whiter than it had been before.

Swearing at me in Italian, he got up and brushed off the snow.

"Why were you hiding there?" he squeaked, "Didn't you see my signal?"

"Sure, I saw it, but I thought you were in trouble and it might be a trap," I replied.

"There wasn't any trouble," he continued, brushing the snow off his legs, "there's no one here except the girl."

"Good, but I didn't know that."

I followed him inside, unable to prevent a large grin, as I pictured his antics when he walked into my gun. Kim stood with her back to me, and the Italian girl was slumped in a chair in front of her. Her dark hair was dishevelled, and her top lip was swollen. There was also a lump under her left eye, which was already beginning to discolour.

Renato spoke first.

"Did she tell you the whole story?"

Kim turned and nodded.

"We've hit the jackpot; they're bringing the professor's daughter down shortly." Pointing at the girl she went on,

"She was about to arrange for a car to meet them at the landing pad."

Renato walked forwards until he was in front of the girl. She shrank back into the chair as he struck her across the face, shouting at her in Italian.

I remembered the night she'd been with Garlic Mouth, when I was worked over at the chalet, but it angered me to see this seemingly unwarranted brutality towards her. This Renato was a vicious little sod alright.

"Where are they headed for?" I asked.

Kim told Renato to stop, as she turned to answer me.

"They're going by car to a lakeside villa, by Lake Maggiore. Sometime tomorrow an agent from the KGB will rendezvous with them. That's all she knows, except that the girl's been told she's being taken to her father."

"So, what do you propose we do?" I asked.

The Italian girl was sitting forwards in the chair crying, and Kim told Renato to back off.

"Listen," she said, "we'll get her to arrange for the car to meet them, so we'll know how to recognise it. Then we'll high tail it off down the valley and pick a spot to block the road with a fake accident. As soon as they stop, we'll jump them."

Renato liked the plan, but I didn't.

"It's pretty risky. I think there's a better way," I said.

"Kim looked at me questioningly.

"What is it?"

"Well, if this girl will tell us where the villa is, we can get there first and surprise them."

Renato clearly didn't like my assuming control, and piped in,

"Suppose there are others at the villa?"

"Well then we'll have to take care of them first, whatever we choose to do there'll be problems, but we'll have the element of surprise."

I could tell Kim favoured my idea, and she turned to Renato.

"Let's find out if this girl knows where it is, and if there's anyone there."

The wench sensed that she was in for another grilling and tried to make it to the door. Renato pounced on her like a fox on a rabbit, and once again his actions did nothing for the poor kid's looks.

Kim pulled him off and they bundled her back into the chair and began questioning her in Italian. She answered them as readily as her swollen lips would allow, and when she'd finished, Kim looked pleased.

"It's an empty villa near Cannero that's closed for the winter. There's no one there, so if we get there first, we can set up a nice welcoming committee. That was a pretty good brainwave you had, Matt."

"Let's hope you still think so this time tomorrow," I replied.

Grabbing the girl, Renato pushed her across to the telephone, and stood by her menacingly while she arranged for the car.

Kim turned to me.

"Matt, you come with me and we'll take the girl with us in her car." Then turning to Renato, she said, "Now the car's been arranged to meet the chopper, you pick up your car and follow us. We should be able to beat them to the villa, in plenty of time to get set up."

The line of Kim's mouth had hardened, now that she felt in charge of the situation. She looked rather less attractive like this, than when her femininity predominated. But this was a tough business and she couldn't afford to be anything but tough.

Thinking about when the others landed, I asked, "Won't this girl be missed?"

The girl's told us she wasn't going to the villa with them," Kim replied.

I nodded.

"Fair enough — let's get going," I said.

Reaching the Fiat, I pushed our captive into the back and climbed in beside her. Renato had tied her hands, but she didn't want to give any trouble. Taking the wheel, Kim drove back to the car park, and we dropped Renato at his car. Shortly afterwards we were speeding down the valley with him following. The sun was going down as we followed the mountain road, twisting its way through the walls of rock on either side. A few miles on, the road was clear of snow and Kim pushed the little car as fast as the frequent corners would allow. I estimated that it was about fifty miles to the villa, so it would be getting dark when we got there.

"I shall have to get some gasoline when we hit the trunk road," Kim called back. "Make sure you keep our little friend quiet; we don't want the plan loused up now."

I glanced at the girl.

"Don't worry, I'll cope," I assured her.

As we swung onto the forecourt of the filling station on the Domodossola-Verbania road, I kept my hand ready to jam it over the girl's mouth, if she attempted to call out, but she remained quiet. Soon afterwards we were speeding off with Renato in hot pursuit.

Chapter 10

My calculations proved correct, and it was almost dark by the time we reached Verbania and turned north along the lake. Twenty minutes later we were entering the outskirts of Cannero Riviera, and Kim slowed the car and spoke to the girl in Italian. I guessed that she was asking for directions to the villa, but the girl didn't answer.

"What's going on back there — you two in a clinch or something?" Kim's voice sounded edgy.

"I never take advantage of a girl when her hands are tied," I threw back. "I think she's asleep."

Kim pulled the car over and stopped. She swore to herself as she groped about for the interior light, and when it came on, she leaned back to see for herself. The girl woke up and sat staring at us, her dark eyes large and frightened. Renato's car pulled up behind, the door slammed, and next moment he opened the door of the Fiat and got in beside Kim.

"Is something wrong?" he asked.

"I need directions to the villa, and our little friend has clammed up," Kim retorted.

Renato swung round and aimed a blow at the girl's face, but before it landed, she had slid down between the seats and began screaming. Then he reached over and struck her with his fist, wherever he could land a blow.

"Hold on a minute!" I shouted at him. "This'll get us nowhere."

He took no notice, so I pushed him back into his seat.

"For Christ's sake, calm down a minute, and let's get this sorted out," I snapped. "Kim — what's this girl babbling about?"

Kim twisted her head towards me.

"She thinks that we intend to kill her as soon as we get to the villa, so she won't give the directions."

I could understand the girl's concern, and I wasn't going to allow that.

"Tell her she'll be okay, and after we get the professor's daughter, we'll let her go."

"You're not giving the orders here!" Renato said savagely, then wrestling his shoulder free from my grip.

"Leave her to me, I'll make her talk," he spat.

"Cool it, both of you," Kim broke in. "I'm running this show and if there's any killing to be done, I'll decide when and who." Her voice was shrill, and although she was trying to sound tough, I could tell that she was feeling shaky.

I pulled the girl back into her seat and Kim spoke softly to her. After a while, the girl responded, and then turned to me as if she wanted my acknowledgement.

"What's happening?" I asked.

Kim spoke with the girl again then turned to me. "She saying she'll show us the way if you promise that she'll be alright."

I looked at the girl then back at Kim.

"I want your word she won't be harmed by us — any of us."

Kim's face softened.

"Do you think I'd kill anyone without provocation?"

"No, not you, but I want Renato's word on it," I told her.

He looked at Kim then smiled at me.

"I was just making the girl co-operative," he said. "I've no wish to kill her."

It didn't add up too much, but it was the best assurance I was likely to get.

Gripping the girl's arm, I felt the plumpness of her flesh beneath the jumper.

"You'll be alright," I told her softly, trying to indicate with my voice and expression what I was saying.

"If you help us, you won't be harmed." I turned back to Kim. "You explain it to her."

They both talked together, and the girl seemed satisfied. Kim drove off, and shortly afterwards we stopped outside a pair of large iron gates that barred our way to a large gravel drive. Renato pulled up behind us and he and Kim examined them. Luckily the locking mechanism was broken and rusty, and they were able to swing them open. Leaving Renato to close them, we continued along the driveway until our headlights picked out the villa at the end of a tree-lined approach.

We had left the last of the snow as soon as we turned along the lake, so there was no worry about us leaving tracks. But we would have to hide the cars before the others arrived. We pulled up, and hustling the girl with me, I followed Kim around the villa to find the best place to gain entry.

Kim flashed her torch along every window, but they were all tightly shuttered and presented a formidable obstacle to our gaining entry. The doors too, proved both heavy and securely locked.

After hiding the cars, Renato had joined us and we completed a circuit of the solid old stone villa, without finding a way to penetrate it.

"It's like a god-damn fortress," Kim grumbled. "If we can't crack it pretty soon, we'll have to hide in the bushes and jump them from out here."

"That will be a lot riskier," I said. "There must be a way in somewhere — let's try the rear again."

As we hurried back through the paved garden to the rear patio, I pushed the girl in front of me, and thought that she must be enjoying our difficulty now we'd arrived here. Reaching the back of the villa, I saw there were two pillars supporting a first-floor balcony. I told Kim to shine the light as I grabbed the gnarled old vine that was twined around them.

I turned to Renato.

"Nip back to the car and get me something I can

force the shutters with," I told him, then said to Kim, "You take care of the girl while I climb up."

Hauling myself over the ornamental railings, I stepped onto the balcony, and even in the dim light I could see that the shutters were metal and couldn't be forced open. Looking up, I saw there was another smaller window above, with what looked like wooden shutters of less solid construction. It was probably that of the servants' quarters.

"Kim, can you shine the light up to that window above?" I asked.

The pale beam filtered through the railings, and rose up the wall to the window, revealing it in detail.

I heard Renato returning, and swearing as he collided with an obstacle in the undergrowth.

"Hurry up!" I called down to him.

He clambered up to join me, and helping him over the railings, I took the large screwdriver and wrench that he'd brought with him. He also had another torch, and by its light we could see that the window only had old wooden shutters that didn't appear tightly fixed.

I tested the creeper that ran up the wall, but it came away in my hand.

"It won't support me," I said, "you'll have to stand on my shoulders and use the creeper to steady yourself against the wall, then I'll try to push you up the rest of the way."

He looked up at the window.

"Okay, but can you hold me long enough for me to

force it?"

"I don't know," I said, "but we'll soon find out, it's our only chance."

"What are you two sons of bitches doing up there for Pete's sake?" came Kim's voice from below.

Renato leaned over the railings and gave her a brief explanation.

"For crying out loud, get on with it then!" Kim called back.

Taking the torch and screwdriver, he stepped onto my back as I crouched forwards. Then I straightened up slowly, as he scrabbled about for a hold on the wall, and supporting himself, he managed to shift his feet onto my shoulders, as I regained an upright position.

"Can you reach it?" I panted.

"Not yet, you'll have to get me higher, before I can get enough leverage."

Gripping his feet and stepping back from the wall, to give myself a better base from which to exert a push, I jerked him upwards to full arm's length. "How's that?" I asked.

"Okay — okay — hold me there, I can reach it now," he said.

I could hear the shutters rattling, as he forced them with the screwdriver. Several minutes passed and my arms began quivering under the strain of the continual exertion, and his weight seemed to increase with every second.

"You'll have to hurry it up, I can't hold you much

longer," I told him.

"Hang on," he said, "they are tougher than we thought, but I think I can do it."

Then came the crack of splintering wood and smashing glass, as he forced the window. Simultaneously there came the noise of a car engine from the end of the driveway.

Renato hauled himself inside, and I gratefully lowered my arms and leaned against the railings, massaging my muscles.

Kim's voice came from below as she came from the front of the villa, pushing the girl in front of her. "Matt, get down here quick — it's them, they're coming through the gates at the end of the drive!"

I swung my leg over the railings and started to climb down.

"Where's Renato?" Kim continued hastily. "We'll have to ambush them in front of the villa, as they get out of the car."

Hanging for a moment, trying to get a foothold, I could see the dim shape of her and the girl below me.

"Renato's inside, he's probably on his way to the front door to let us in," I called down.

"Oh shit! What a screw up!" Kim's voice was panicky. "Quick, get down here and hold the girl."

With that, her shadow disappeared into the undergrowth, as she made off towards the front of the villa.

She had left the girl for me to grab, and as I started

down the creeper suddenly gave way, and I fell the rest of the distance to the ground. Toppling over, I lost balance.

"Fuck the bush," I swore as its prickly branches grazed my face. "A bloody fine caper this has turned out to be."

Crawling out, still mouthing abuse, I heard the gravel drive crunching as the car approached. The beam from its lights played briefly among the trees as it swung round in front of the villa and disappeared from my view.

I looked for the girl, but she was gone, so I quickly made my way towards the front. The car had stopped, and by the time I reached the corner, the doors were opening. From its lights I could make out four figures moving about in front of the villa.

Feeling for my pistol, I crouched among the shrubbery and slowly edged my way forwards.

Three of the figures were in front of the door, and one was holding a smaller figure that I guessed was the professor's daughter.

Then there was a shout in Italian, which I thought at first was Kim making a challenge, but quickly realised it was the Italian girl shouting a warning to them. A flash, and the crack of revolver shots came next, and one of the figures staggered. As more shots followed, the group piled against the front door, and I couldn't shoot for fear of hitting the professor's daughter. There was a confusion of movement as someone ran to join the group by the door, then two figures were running towards me.

The group by the door disappeared inside, and there were more shots and angry shouts from within.

"Matt — Matt — where are you?"

It was Kim's voice.

"Over here!" I replied, and Kim came towards me dragging a figure behind her.

Pushing the figure at me, Kim panted, "Take care of her, Matt. I'm going back to help Renato."

Before I could answer, she had turned and was running back towards the villa.

I grabbed the figure and saw it was a girl. I couldn't make out her features but could tell she was a youngster.

"What's happening?" she asked, her voice weak and confused. "I'm all mixed up."

"Don't worry, kid, you'll be alright," I assured her as she fell against me.

Kim had reached the doorway and disappeared inside, as I heard a staccato of more shots together with breaking glass and excited shouts in Italian.

Realising that if Kim and Renato came off worse, I would be a dead duck when the kidnappers came out, I decided that I must get to them and balance up their disadvantage.

Shaking the girl firmly, I said,
"Now listen. You stay here and keep quiet. You'll be alright, and I'll be right back." She stiffened. "You understand — don't move from here."

I left her and made off for the front door. I was

almost there when someone emerged and fired a shot back through the doorway. Straining my eyes to see who it was, I levelled my pistol. If it was one of the gang, I could pick him off before he got wise. Then I saw it was Kim's slim figure, as she crouched by the open door. Running the remaining distance, I dropped down beside her.

"You alright, Kim?"

"Yes, Matt, but Renato's been shot, he's still inside, hurt bad. We'll have to make a run for it, where's the girl?"

"I left her in the bushes and told her not to move."

A bullet thudded into the woodwork beside us.

"What about the Italian bitch?" Kim asked.

"Christ, I'd forgotten about her," I replied. "She gave me the slip."

"It was her that raised the alarm," Kim said, trying to pull the door shut as she spoke.

"If we can swing this shut, the key's in it and we can lock them in, it'll give us a few minutes' start."

"Come out of the way, let me try - you cover me," I said.

The large old hinges were stiff, and it was difficult to get enough leverage without getting my head blown off. Pulling Kim back, I moved closer to get a better grip, and felt the heavy panelling begin to move as I pulled against its weight.

"It's moving!" I whispered.

Two more bullets whistled past, and the shots

sounded pretty close. Then the door swung shut and Kim leaped up and turned the key with a loud clunk.

I straightened up to join her, and two more bullets smashed into the stonework beside me. These had come from someone outside and ducking low I brought my pistol round to fire back, as I glimpsed a figure running towards the car. Before I could level it, Kim had fired and the figure stopped abruptly, then sprawled full length on the gravel.

"Quick - the car!" Kim shouted. We both sprinted forwards, and she reached it first and dived in behind the wheel.

"The key's here, find the professor's daughter - hurry, Matt."

Making for the bushes where I'd left her, I heard the engine start, and the sound of wheel spin on the gravel, as Kim turned the car in a tight circle on the driveway.

Reaching the spot where I'd left the girl, I realised she wasn't there. I didn't know her name to call her and I began swearing at the mix up.

The car skidded to a halt at the edge of the garden, and the full beam of its headlights splayed among the bushes.

"Move it, Matt, they'll be on us in a minute," Kim shouted anxiously.

"There's no one here, she must have wandered off," I called back. "Sod the girl!"

Plunging deeper into the bushes, I could see a

shadowy figure on the ground beside a tree.

Three steps and I was bending over it. It was her, and pocketing my pistol I grabbed her arm, swung it round my neck, and with my other arm encircling her small waist, I carried her through the undergrowth towards the car.

Kim flung open the rear door, and pushing the girl inside, I was about to follow when shouts came from the corner of the villa. A bullet ricocheted off the ground beside me and I felt another hit the sole of my boot like a sledgehammer. Diving forwards onto the girl, we both fell across the back seat as the car roared away, careering off down the driveway.

I was still struggling to get properly into the car when it screeched to a halt, rolling me into the foot well between the seats.

"Jesus Christ!" I protested. "What the bloody hell are you doing?"

"The gates! Open the gates!" Kim was shouting.

Scrambling about, I managed to push myself out feet first, and running to the gates I felt the unevenness of the boot that had been hit by the bullet.

As I threw open the gates, Kim drove through, and before the car had stopped, I swung open the front passenger door and leaped in. It flew shut of its own accord from the acceleration, as we raced forwards into the night.

"We've made it," I panted, feeling elated. "That'll give the bastards something to think about."

"We're not clear yet," Kim replied, "besides we've lost Renato."

My jubilation faded. In the excitement I'd forgotten about him.

Kim slowed the car as we approached the main road.

"Where are we heading?" I asked her. "The shortest route to the border is along the lake."

"We're not heading for the border. I've got different instructions."

I was about to ask her what they were, when there was a loud rubbing noise from the rear, and the car bumped along, slowing down.

Kim was having difficulty steering.

"We've got a flat," I said. "Try to make it to those streetlights and I'll take a look."

We had reached the outskirts of the town and there were several lamps where we halted.

"I hope there's a spare wheel and a jack," I said, climbing out.

The offside rear tyre was squashed flat to the rim and I kicked it as Kim joined me.

"A bullet must have got it," I said. "It's tubeless or it wouldn't have lasted this far."

"The trunk's locked," Kim said, and went back to get the ignition key. As she raised the lid, I was relieved to see the shape of the spare, and pulling back the cover, I removed it from its cradle. A jack and wheel brace were clipped behind it.

"Will you have enough time to change it, Matt?

Kim asked anxiously.

"Yes, even if they saw us turn this way, we've got their car, and if they find ours, they can't start them."

Prizing off the wheel trim, I fitted the brace and pushed it down with my boot to loosen the nuts. Then I groped under the chassis for the jacking point but couldn't locate it. Lying full length on the ground with my head under the car, the jacking point was just visible, and the metal jack clanked against the lug as I rammed it home.

Next, the rear door opened, and the professor's daughter started getting out, stepping on me as she did. Grabbing her foot, I began pushing her back.

"Let go of me!" she screamed, lashing out with her feet.

"Kim, take care of this kid will you, I've got enough to do down here," I grumbled.

Removing the flat, I fitted the spare and removed the jack. Throwing them in the boot, I slammed the lid. Turning to get in the car, I saw headlights approaching from the direction of the villa.

"Matt - quick - I think it's them!" Kim shouted.

As her warning came a bullet whined past my ear as a shot rang out.

Diving flat, I slithered round to join Kim and the girl who were already crouching by the front wing.

"They must have taken Renato's keys and found his car," Kim panted.

Everything then happened at once. The professor's daughter broke away and began running along the street.

There was a shout, and someone began running after her. Kim levelled her gun but didn't fire for fear of hitting the girl. I was wrestling desperately with my anorak pocket to remove my pistol, which was entangled with the lining. Next a large figure appeared from around the car and confronted me.

I froze and waited for the bullet.

It never came.

Instead I was grabbed roughly by his free hand and pushed back towards Kim.

Covering us with his gun, he hissed something in Italian, and Kim began raising her arms. She hesitated for a moment, then the gun fell from her fingers as her arms continued upwards.

Along the road there was a brief struggle beneath a streetlamp, and then her assailant came towards us, pushing the girl in front of him.

Our man picked up Kim's gun and tore mine from my anorak pocket, then he motioned for us both to get in the car, and moments later the professor's daughter was bundled into the back with us.

After some conversation together, outside the car, I recognised the Italian girl as she entered the passenger's seat. She spoke to the big man who'd squeezed in behind the wheel, and he handed her his gun. As we drove off, he turned briefly and said something to us. I saw his thick lips part in a sadistic grin. I didn't understand what he said but knew that I wouldn't feel any better if I had. As he turned away, the only thing remaining was the strong smell of garlic.

Chapter 11

Huddled in the back of the car, my mind raced through what had happened. Victory had been snatched away from us just as success was in our grasp.

I was frightened.

Frightened of what was about to happen to Kim and myself, without us having the slightest chance of making a fight for it.

I was angry too.

Angry at not being able to level the score with Garlic Mouth, and bitter in the knowledge that all my suffering, and the soldier's death, had all been for nothing.

I was about to reach over and try to throttle him from behind, chancing a bullet from the Italian girl when we reached the villa gates and drove through onto the driveway. The other car was waiting inside, as we drove on and pulled up at the front door.

We were pushed out at gunpoint and ushered into the large hallway, which was illuminated by a solitary light at the far end. A wide, stone staircase led off to one side, flanked by a heavily ornamented handrail. Around the marbled ground floor, six or seven panelled doors led into rooms.

Garlic Mouth called the other driver, whose name was Chino, and he came inside, closing the door. After exchanging a few words, they checked the windows, then switched on the lighting.

A huge chandelier showered brilliance all around the hall, and I took in as much of the layout as I could, including a quick survey of the top landing and several other doors. I couldn't see any signs of the previous gun battle, but it was a large, solid mansion and only a detailed examination would have found any bullet holes.

Kim was standing in front of me with the professor's daughter, and as our eyes met, I could see she was worried about what would happen next.

We didn't have long to wait. Chino came across to us.

"So, your little plan has failed," he said in English. "And now I suppose you are wondering what will happen to you."

He moved closer to Kim, and using the muzzle of his revolver, prodded her savagely in the lower abdomen. She winced at the pain, bending forwards slightly but remained silent.

Chino smiled gloatingly.

"We will have to think of something *VERY* special for such a beauty as you," he said, his rat-like eyes glinting with perverted pleasure, as he contemplated the idea.

It was my turn next for his attentions.

I was ready for the belly prod and tensed my

167

abdominals before it came, but it still hurt and I wondered how Kim had taken it unprepared, without crying out.

"As for you my friend, I hope you are a good swimmer — especially underwater." He paused, relishing our helplessness, then went on. "Parts of this lake are said to have sunken treasure. Unfortunately, it's so deep that no one has ever succeeded in finding it, but perhaps you will have time for a quick look when we deposit you on the bottom."

He grinned and jammed the gun into me a couple more times for good measure.

I'd like to choke the living daylights out of you, you rat-faced bastard, I thought, but remained silent.

As his death sentence penetrated my anger, it wasn't difficult to show fear in my face as he looked at me, and I hoped he would play along for a while to get his kicks. Where there's life there's hope, I thought, and our only chance was to play for time.

Chino turned his attention back to Kim.

"But first you will answer some questions."

With that, Garlic Mouth grabbed Kim from behind and began dragging her across to a large heavy-legged table. As Chino followed, I stepped forwards but was halted by the Italian girl, who pointed her revolver at my head.

Kim struggled valiantly but was eventually overpowered by the combined weight of the two men, who finally succeeded in getting her spread-eagled across the table.

Chino tore some cords from the heavy curtains and secured her hands, one to each table leg.

Throwing his body across her, Garlic Mouth crushed Kim to the table, as Chino struggled with her legs until they were tied by the ankles to the table legs on the other side. Kim was now helplessly spread upwards across the table, her head hanging over one edge, and her legs bent over the other end where her ankles were tied.

Leaving her, they advanced to me and pushed me into a chair. After tying me to it, they dragged me across to the centre of the hall.

Going back to Kim, they called to the Italian girl to help, and pushed the table across the hall floor next to me. Grabbing Kim's arms, Chino and Garlic Mouth stretched them out tightly, pulling her body to full stretch, and re-tied her wrists to the table legs.

Straightening up, Garlic Mouth looked towards me and said something to Chino.

Chino grinned as he spoke to me.

"Now you will see how brave your beautiful friend can be."

The menace in his voice sent a shiver through me, and I felt a cold sweat exuding from my body.

Turning back to Kim's upturned body, he released the waistband of her ski-pants, slid the zip down, and despite her efforts to avoid it by squirming as much as she could, he dragged them down to below her knees, leaving her lower body unclothed except for her brief underwear.

Garlic Mouth leaned over her, and sliding his hands beneath her buttocks, he lifted them from the table, as Chino pulled down her briefs, leaving her naked from the waist down, to where her clothes hung over her ankles.

Enjoying their work, they then took each of her legs and re-tied them again, so that her buttocks were resting on the table's edge, thrusting her pelvic region upwards, revealing her femininity in a taut, sensuous outline.

The firmness of her buttocks moulded perfectly with the softness of the V-shaped region between the fold of her upper thighs, and as she continued to struggle, her movements emphasised the beauty of her young body, stretched in erotic posture. As I watched her lovely body being revealed in this way, Chino began moving his hands upwards along the inside of her thighs, as he bent over her.

A mad rage consumed me, and I pulled violently at the cords that bound me, in a vain attempt to free myself. Nothing they could do to me mattered now if I could only free myself long enough to have a go at them.

"You sadistic bastards," I shouted, and went on hurling abuse at them, as I struggled desperately to free myself.

They paid me no attention as I cursed them, then Chino spoke to Kim.

"You will tell us precisely who you are, and from where

you receive your instructions." His voice was calm, and he spoke with the deliberation of a practised interrogator. Kim remained silent and moving his hand closer into the V between her spread-eagled thighs, he spoke again.

"Perhaps you did not understand - I will repeat the question."

He asked her again, and again it remained unanswered.

As he moved in front of her, I thought at first that I would have to sit helpless and witness her being raped, but this wasn't his intention, at least not yet. Instead he moved his hand again, and grasping her pubic hair, he brutally twisted it until the pale skin at the side of her vagina was stretched, as he cruelly pulled the hairs.

Kim cried out, and at the same time one of my hands came free, and I launched myself forwards attempting to grab the gun from the Italian girl, as she stood watching them. She jumped back out of reach, and Garlic Mouth advanced on me, knocking me sideways onto the floor. Using my free hand, I struggled to untie the other hand, but I was struck again and dragged upright, where they twisted my free arm behind the chair and tied it again.

Garlic Mouth drew a knife, and releasing the catch, sprung it open, and I thought he was going to finish me. Instead he turned back to Kim and prodding the tip against the curve of her naked abdomen, he held it there menacingly as he spoke excitedly in Italian.

Next moment there was a sound of a car pulling up

on the gravel driveway outside the front door.

As the others heard it, they stood silent for a moment looking from one to the other.

Garlic Mouth moved first. Rapidly giving instructions, he cut me free and then freed Kim's arms and legs. She slid off the table and hastily replaced her clothes, as the Italian girl and Chino pushed us along the hall with the professor's daughter, to a large panelled door beneath the stairs. He beckoned to us with his gun to go in, as Garlic Mouth crossed to the front door. Chino switched on the light and it revealed a stone stairway that led down to a cellar. Once inside, he swung the door shut and locked it, then holstering his gun, he produced a knife from an inside pocket and grabbed the professor's daughter.

She whimpered as he roughly pulled back the hair behind her head, jerking her chin upwards. The blade of the knife sprang open with a lethal sounding click, as he pressed the sharp edge against her upwardly stretched throat.

The Italian girl's gun held Kim and me at bay from our position on the stone steps, and we could do nothing but stand and watch.

"Don't make a sound," Chino hissed, just loud enough for us to hear, "or this one gets it first."

I looked at Kim and could tell that she knew as well as I that he would carry out his threat.

I could faintly hear voices and guessed it was coming from a conversation at the front door.

We waited in silence for several minutes, after which I heard the sound of a car engine that faded away as the front door was closed.

Chino released his grip on the girl and pushed her down towards us. Then unlocking the door, he went back into the hallway. The Italian girl followed, and transferring the key to the outside, she closed the door and locked it.

I turned to Kim. "You alright?"

"Yes, Matt — just a bit shaken."

There's no sign of Renato, do you think he got away?" I asked.

Kim looked at me, "No he was hurt too bad to go far."

I held her to me and patted her back as she leaned against me. She rested her head on my shoulder and standing there together we seemed to gain strength from each other. Then she stiffened, as she looked at the professor's daughter. The kid was crying again and must have been traumatised after all she'd been through in the last few days.

"It's alright," Kim said, consoling the girl, as she went to her and held her in a maternal embrace. They spoke to each other for a while and I heard Kim say, "Everything will be alright, Helen, you must be brave."

I went past them on the steps and down into the cellar. It was cold and felt damp as I reached the bottom. Several bare electric light bulbs shone dimly as they hung from the ceiling at intervals, between row upon row of stacked bottles. In the first avenue I found a set of switches on the side of the old stone archway. Flicking them all down simultaneously, a flood of light revealed a winery of astonishing proportions.

I called to Kim to come down with Helen and went back to meet them.

Kim spoke first.

"By what I could hear, Matt, that was the Carabinieri outside."

"Well if it was, they didn't stay long, and we couldn't do anything about it anyway," I replied.

Kim nodded then went on,

"Perhaps they heard the shooting and were investigating."

"Maybe," I said, "it could be why the others panicked and hustled us down here, but it's too late now."

Our voices echoed strangely in the stone archways of the vault. I couldn't even estimate the number of bottles that were stacked on the thick wooden trestles, but it must have been thousands.

"Listen Kim, there might be another way out of here. You and Helen stick together and make your way down this side, and I'll take the alley on the left. If one of us finds something give a call. Get a move on while we still have time."

The alley on my side turned abruptly, then continued for about twenty yards. The piles of bottles became less in number as I continued, until there were only a dozen or so on each trestle. All of them were encrusted with the grime of age and must have lain undisturbed for many years.

At this end of the passage it was darker, as the bulb that hung from the half-circled ceiling hadn't lit up. My ski boots clomped loudly on the uneven flagstones, as I continued to the last of the wine racks. The trestle at the end had no bottles on it, but there was a large bundle that in the dim light looked to be a roll of old carpet. Beyond this, in a stone recess, was a large, solid door with iron fittings that I knew, even before I examined it, there was no chance of forcing open.

"Matt." Kim was calling from the other end. Turning to answer her, I could see the bundle on the rack more clearly. It was an old carpet tied with a rope at each end. I called to Kim to join me, then thinking that the ropes might be useful in some way, I reached over and began untying the one nearest to me.

"What have you found, Matt? Is there a way out?"

"No, but there's something here, give me a hand."

Kim touched my arm as she stood beside me,

"What is it, Matt?"

"I don't know yet."

We pulled at the tightly rolled end and I felt down inside. My fingers felt a smooth, hard object, and pulling it clear I saw it was a large stone. Holding the carpet open, I peered in. It was too dark to see what was farther down, so stretching my arm I reached in again. The frayed edges of the carpet pressed against my face as my hands groped inside.

I then felt hair, and a pair of ears, as I encircled the top of someone's head with my fingers. It was still warm, and forcing my arm down, I gripped some clothing by the neck. "There's a body in here, Kim!" I said.

I exerted all the grip I could muster and pulled. A body slid along towards me, and Renato's head appeared, his eyes staring blankly up at me.

"Oh my God!" Kim gasped and half slumped against me.

I pushed his body back, and we stood for a moment gathering our thoughts.

"Matt, I'm scared, if we can't get out of here were done for."

"Take it easy," I said, trying to sound reassuring. "This has been weighted ready to dump in the lake so there must be some rear exit. That door over there won't budge, so if that's it we're sunk."

I realised as I said it that my choice of words could have been better, if they were meant to console her.

"What did you find down the other passage?" I asked.

Kim drew in a deep breath and braced herself. "It's no use, Matt, the way's barred by a big iron grille."

"Isn't there a door in it?"

"Yes, there is a door, but it's heavy and locked."

"Come on," I said, "let's take a look."

Helen was halfway down the other passage, looking dazed and only vaguely aware of what was going on.

I shook her gently. "Come on, Helen, we're going to find a way out of here."

My intention to buck her up had as much effect as a flea bite on a rhinoceros, so I shook her harder as my impatience took over.

"Pull yourself together, kid, we're pushed for time," I said, pushing her along in front of me.

As we reached the iron grille, I could see that it completely blocked the tunnel.

In the middle was a heavy iron door, with a formidable looking lock on one side that pinned it through a slot in the surrounding framework.

"This place is built like a bloody fortress," I swore.

I could see about twenty or thirty feet beyond the grille, where both sides were stacked with cardboard boxes, which looked like cases of wine ready for delivery, and other boxes that could be cartons of cigarettes.

"You know what I think, Kim?"

"No, what?" She turned her face towards me, and despite everything I thought how lovely she was.

"This old villa is used for smuggling. It's right by the lake and I'll bet there's a jetty beyond this tunnel." I cast my eyes around to find something to use on the door, as I spoke.

Kim turned from peering at the boxes.

"You could be right. This lake runs up into Switzerland and the border's not far. It's two miles wide, and on a dark night a boat could easily slip through."

I spotted a wooden pole and began ramming through the bars that held the lock. As I exerted pressure, the pole broke, catapulting me backwards

"F — f — f — sod the pole!" I blurted, managing to stifle my language.

"When are we going home, I'm frightened of this place — please take me home," Helen was pleading.

"It's alright, Helen, we'll be going before long," Kim tried to assure her.

Further effort here was useless, as the solid grille wouldn't budge.

"I'm going back to look at that other door, it might—" I stopped in midsentence.

There was someone coming!

Grabbing the two pieces of broken pole, I thrust one piece towards Kim.

"This is it, Kim, but we're not going out without a fight. Get behind the barrels on your side, and when they' get near, we'll come out swinging." We scrambled back and I waited with Helen in behind me.

The sound of footsteps and muffled voices echoed through the tunnel. Then I realised they were not coming from the steps to the villa, but from along the tunnel beyond the iron grille.

Of course!

It came to me in a flash. Those upstairs wouldn't have had the time to prepare Renato for his watery grave. This must have been done by more of the gang that were working down here when we first arrived.

Hope flashed through me, as it dawned on me that this was the pall bearers coming back for his body. What's more, they wouldn't know that we had been locked down here when the police came.

My heart raced with excitement at the thought of this chance. When they came through to this side, we could surprise them.

I crouched in readiness and motioned to Kim, as the seconds ticked by and the footsteps got nearer.

Next moment, two men in dark jackets and caps turned a corner and appeared in view. Walking towards us through the avenue of boxes, they suddenly stopped when they saw that the lights from our side were on. I cursed silently. I'd forgotten about the lights!

The larger of the two men spoke to the other man, who shrugged and then continued towards the grille. Producing a key from his pocket, he inserted it into the lock. The big chap started to argue, but the one with the key was obviously in charge and unlocking the door, he stepped through. As the big one followed, he drew a gun from his jacket and they both moved onto our side of the grille.

I moved forwards for a better position to jump them, and my damaged ski boot became hooked on the leg of the trestle. As I freed it, the noise alerted the two men, and the one with the gun turned in my direction and levelled it ready to shoot.

I couldn't have arranged it better had I done it deliberately. Seizing the opportunity, Kim moved silently out, and swinging her pole in a full half circle she struck the big man across the back of his head. He dropped to the floor, his gun rattling along the flagstones as he fell. As I jumped out in front of the other man, he tried to raise his arm to ward off my blow but never made it. I struck him with a shattering blow to the side of the head. He fell in a heap on top of the other man, and both remained motionless.

Kim grabbed up the gun and began searching the two men. Helen was sitting on the floor, and I turned to her.

"Jump up, kid, we're going," I said. "Come on, we're getting out of here."

She still seemed drugged and stooping to pick her up I caught a whiff of her breath, which smelled awful.

"I don't know what they pumped into you, Helen, but don't worry, kid, you'll be alright soon," I told her.

She obeyed me meekly as I stood her up, but when we reached the grille, she fell against it, and said something to me in German that I didn't understand. Then she was sick, and I knew what it was she told me.

Leaving her, I joined Kim, beside the bodies of the two men.

"Helen's in a bad way," I said, "she's coming out of the drugs and throwing up." Then, looking at our victims, I asked,

"Are they dead?

Kim finished her search and straightened up.

"No, but the one I zapped has probably got a

fractured skull, and your poor sonovabitch will need some false teeth."

I grinned as I asked,

"Find anything?"

"Nothing of use, except the gun."

"You keep it," I said, "I'll hang on to Helen — let's get going."

There was the sound of footsteps descending the stone steps, and it echoed along the alleyway. There was no mistaking the direction this time. Our captors were coming down.

"Quick, Matt," Kim whispered, "you take Helen through the door and I'll close it."

I grabbed the girl and we both stumbled through, as Kim followed and began swinging the door shut. Shouts came from along the rows of barrels, and, as she struggled to lock it, a shot rang out and echoed wildly around the cellar walls.

"Kim — get away from that grille!" I shouted.

"It's jammed — I can't lock it, Matt."

Leaving Helen, I turned back and pulled Kim aside. The others were running towards us between the rows of trestles. Another shot rang out and a bullet struck one of the iron bars beside me and ricocheted around the walls.

Kim levelled the gun she'd taken and fired a shot that halted their advance.

As they hastily took up positions behind the wine casks, I was able to wiggle the key into the right position, and securely lock the door. I removed the key, and the three of us raced off along the rows of boxes. More bullets whined by us as we reached the intersection, and we turned the corner and paused for breath.

"You alright?" I asked Kim.

"A bit out of breath," she panted, "I must be getting overweight — remind me to diet when we get out of here."

"When this is done, I'll buy you the biggest dinner you've ever had," I said, "and after that we'll both go to bed for a week and sleep it off."

"You're on," she replied, "providing we don't spend all the time sleeping."

I laughed.

"The power of nature is a wonderful thing, to make two people think of sex at a time like this," I said.

As the tensions of the previous hours eased slightly, we both chuckled and relaxed, in our moment of safety.

Chapter 12

Further down the passageway, we bolted a connecting door and began to feel safe. It was much wider here, and each side was stacked with thousands of cartons. Parked beside them were several trolleys, and in the main assembly area was a small forklift truck, which was obviously used to move the boxes. Beyond this was a large up-and-over metal door of heavy construction, set into the wall, and beside it was a press button starter switch.

Kim was first to speak.

"This kidnap's only a sideshow for this gang. They must be running a terrific contraband business from here."

"You're damn right — this looks like a big Mafia operation, and we're up against a bigger outfit than we bargained for."

Kim didn't answer, but I knew that the thought didn't please her any more than it did me.

Helen was managing to stay on her feet but was far from well.

Kim checked her gun.

"The longer we stay here the less chance we have. If that button controls the door, we'll have to make a break for it."

I knew she was right, but I didn't fancy meeting what might be on the other side.

"Okay but switch off the lights before we open the door," I said. I drew Helen to one side as Kim flicked off the lights, and we stood in silence for a few moments, as our eyes adjusted to the darkness.

"I'm operating the door now, Matt — if anyone tries to rush us, I'll use what's left in the gun, and then it's hand to hand."

"Okay, let's do it." I pushed Helen behind me as I spoke, and little beads of perspiration began trickling down my forehead.

The low hum of the electric motor throbbed, and the door began to open upwards.

Straining my eyes, I peered into the darkness. A rectangle of murky gloom started taking shape, till finally there was a click as the motor cut out, and the area of greyness remained constant. I pressed Helen against the wall and waited. Nothing happened.

"We won't be seen till we step outside," Kim whispered. "I'll go first and make a run for the nearest cover."

"Hold on," I said, as I began to make out the blurry outlines outside, "it's best we keep together."

"No, I'll go first," she insisted, "if nothing happens you and Helen can follow."

I tried to protest, but she found my hand in the darkness and pressed the gun into it.

"Take the gun and cover me," she said.

My fingers closed on it as she released her grip, and then she was gone.

I tried to see her whereabouts as the gloom became clearer, then came a shout and the sound of people running about. Then someone was running towards me.

"Close the door quick Matt — it's me."

I felt for the button and the motor hummed into life. As the door closed, I switched on the lights.

Kim stood panting.

"There's several of them out there," she said, panting between breaths. "They saw me, but I managed to duck them."

"I wonder why they didn't shoot?" I asked.

"Maybe they think that if they start a shooting match it'll attract attention from people not connected to the racket," she answered.

That made sense. They wouldn't want to draw attention to this place from the authorities; they'd already got away with it once tonight.

Helen had moved along the cellar and was sitting on a trolley.

Then an idea came to me.

"If we can get that fork-lift truck started, we could use it to get out of here," I said. "Come on, let's take a look."

It was the electric type, commonly used in warehouses and started easily. Kim began operating it forwards and back.

"Get Helen on board and we'll line up with the door," she said.

I sat Helen beside the controls, and we outlined our plan.

Kim would take the gun and drive, and I would switch off the lights and push the door button. Then I'd jump aboard, and that would leave Helen between us.

I found a length of metal tubing that I could use to ward off anyone who tried to jump us, and Kim had the gun to use on her side.

"Right," I said, "are you sure you can operate this thing?"

"I'm okay, kill the lights and open up."

I judged the distance to the truck, then flicked the lights off and pressed the door button.

"Let's go!" I said, scrambling aboard in the darkness.

The truck jerked forwards and the night air caressed my face, as we went out into the greyness. A thick cold mist hung in the air, and Kim's night vision was better than mine, as she drove forwards into the night. Suddenly we were bumping along on a series of ridges, and Helen slid down onto the floor between us.

"Can you see anything?" I asked.

"I thought I could, but now I've lost it — what the hell's this surface we're on?"

We slowed to a halt and heard someone shouting. Next a strong beam of light stabbed out through the swirling mist and swung in an arc towards us. As it penetrated the patchy fog, I could see that we had been bumping along a jetty that formed a small harbour. A motor launch was shining a searchlight along the jetty towards us, and I could see three men running towards us from the harbour.

"Hold tight, I'm going back!" Kim shouted. She swung the truck around, and the manoeuvre caught them by surprise. She rammed the man on her side, who disappeared from view and the other two tried to jump at me. I thrust the metal pipe into the groin of the first man, and he gasped and fell away. The second man grabbed the pipe and hauled himself up beside me. I wrestled to free it from his grip, and as we came together face to face in the glare of the searchlight, I could see it was Chino. His free arm came around and I glimpsed the knife too late and tensed myself for the shock of its impact. The blade tore through my anorak, grazing my ribs. As he withdrew it for another stab, I grabbed his wrist, and we toppled sideways onto the jetty. We hit the ground with me on top, and I smashed my fist into his upturned face. He struggled desperately to push me off, but I held on, striking him several more savage blows.

I felt him sag and drop the knife. I got up and kicked him viciously over the edge. As his body splashed into the lake, I sucked my bleeding knuckles, and was joined by Kim and Helen.

"I hope he finds that bloody treasure," I said.

"We'll have to run for it." Kim said hastily, and grabbing Helen, made off back along the jetty.

Sprinting after them I caught up near the end, and we ran forwards out of range of the searchlight.

The fog was lifting, and we could see much better.

"Make for the front of the villa where the cars are," I shouted.

Racing on ahead, I hoped to get one of them started. Reaching the front, I drew a couple of breaths, then ran to the car that stood in front. It was the big saloon, but the key wasn't there. Swearing loudly, I slammed the door, as Kim dragged Helen to join me.

"This one's no good," I said, "and the other one's not here — we'll have to beat it down the drive to the main road."

I looked anxiously at the villa for any signs of pursuers, as Kim joined me. She drew a deep breath. "I'm pooped, I can't drag Helen much further."

"I'll take her," I said. "Come on, we haven't much time, we've got to make that road."

Grabbing Helen's hand, I gave her a tug that must have come close to dislocating her shoulder, and we started off along the driveway. I was in no mood for niceties and didn't care if my grip hurt her so long as she followed behind me. Halfway down, a narrow road led off to the right, to what looked like a row of garages. I hadn't spotted them before, and I stopped for Kim to catch up.

"What's up?" she panted.

"It looks like some garages over there — come on."

Without waiting, I ran off, still pulling Helen, who

was finding it more and more difficult to stay on her feet, but Kim came alongside and took her other arm which made things easier.

The garages were the open car port type, and I went into the first one, but it was empty. I was about to enter the second when Kim shouted a warning. "Look out!"

A man from inside sprang towards me. I lowered my shoulder and butted him with my head, as we piled against the wall. Kim found the lights, and as we stood there, she threatened him with her gun.

He wasn't armed and was probably a chauffeur or mechanic. He cowered back at the sight of Kim.

She spoke to him in Italian, and he produced some keys from his pocket and handed them to her.

She nodded towards the car that stood there, "Quick, see if they fit."

It looked like the Alfa that Chino had used and opening the door, I wiggled the key into the ignition. "It's okay, it fits."

Kim pushed him into a metal locker and slammed the narrow door. Pausing to lock it, she grabbed Helen and came to the car. Pushing the girl into the back, she jumped into the passenger's seat as I fired the engine and drove out. I flicked on the lights and accelerated away towards the main driveway but saw at once that another car was coming from the villa towards us.

"It's them!" I said.

Spinning the wheel, I threw the car into a tight turn, leaving the tarmac, and ploughing through the garden, just missing a tree that would have put paid to our escape. The wheels of the Alfa spun madly in the soft earth, and as we careered along in a series of broadsides, I fought for control.

"Make for the back — behind the garages — I think there's another road there." Kim's voice was sporadic, as she held herself in the seat and shouted to me.

Straightening out, the little Alfa clung to the ground tenaciously as I headed through the bushes, mowing them down, and knocking aside the larger branches that scraped along the car with a terrific noise. Regaining the road, I made off in the direction that Kim had indicated. The other car had tried to follow me through the garden but had either hit something or was stuck in the soft ground. I could see by a glimpse in the rear mirror; their headlights were at a standstill.

"Swing to the left, Matt — the road's over there," Kim called.

I saw the faint shine of the tarmac as we bumped onto the narrow road. "I hope this leads to the main gate," I shouted back. Squinting ahead for a glimpse of the main entrance, I realised our beam of light wasn't as bright. "We must have smashed a headlight in those bushes," I said. "It's going to make fast driving difficult."

Kim had twisted around and was helping Helen into her seat. Turning back, she spoke to me.

"The poor kid's just been sick."

I cut her short.

"There's the gates and they're open — we've made

it."

I glanced in the mirror to confirm there was no one following, and then turning onto the main road, I swung right, taking the opposite direction from before.

"Where are you going?" Kim asked quickly, "This is the wrong direction for Ghedi."

"Where?" I countered.

"Ghedi — it's a NATO base and my orders are to get Helen there," Kim threw back.

"Well, we're not heading that way." I said firmly. "When the others come after us, they'll most likely assume that we've gone that way. Our best bet is through the mountains to Domodossola, and then to the border."

"Don't be a damn fool, Matt," Kim said angrily, "I've got my orders so turn 'round while there's still time."

"Nothing doing," I said, "I've been beaten up, knifed and shot at, and bloody nearly dumped in the lake, and I'm fed up with it, so we're going my way!"

"Look, Matt," Kim said appealingly, "it's been rough on me too but we've made it this far, and if we get the kid back to my people, we'll have pulled off a great triumph for the West, otherwise it will all have been for nothing."

"No dice," I countered. "I'm making for the Swiss border and she can be handed over to the Swiss authorities."

"What about you?" she said. "You will have to tell

them everything."

"I've thought about that, and I figure if I make a clean breast of it, they'll believe that the soldier's death was really an unfortunate accident."

Kim was quiet for several seconds before she spoke again.

"Stop the car Matt, I want to tell something, and after you've heard what I have to say, I'll be willing to leave it up to you."

Her voice was softer now, almost pleading, but I took no notice. She leaned towards me and rested her hand on mine, as I changed gear to negotiate a tight bend.

"Please Matt, it's important that you know the whole story before it's too late." She paused, then went on. "I promise you won't regret it once you hear what I have to say."

I found the car slowing as my foot eased off the pedal, and I knew she'd hooked me. Spotting a lay-by, I swung the car off the road and pulled up.
"Okay, let's have it," I said.

She twisted to face me as I doused the lights, and I could feel her nearness in the darkness. She found my hand again and held it gently, entwining her fingers in mine, letting them rest on my thigh. I could faintly make out the shape of her head and shoulders and felt a strong sexual urge spreading through my body.

"When you first came to my room with your story," she began, "I contacted my superior, and he decided to get you to help us. His plan was to get your help, by me telling you that we would assist you with your problem about that soldier."

My interest deepened.

"Go on," I said.

"Well his plan worked, and from the moment we met I sensed there was a chemistry between us. It sounds corny but it happens sometimes, and I think you felt it too."

She waited for me to answer. I searched my mind for the truth, as I mulled over the past days.

"Like you say," I said, "it sounds corny, but it happens."

The grip of our fingers tightened as we looked at each other through the darkness that divided us.

Kim was speaking again.

"I almost blew the plan and told you the truth there and then. It was as much as I could do not to level with you, for I felt sure that you would still help us."

"What do you mean — level with me about the truth?"

"It's about that young soldier," she said quietly.

"Well, what about him?"

"You didn't kill him."

"What do you mean I didn't kill him? There was no one else there, and I hit him and made off with the truck."

"I know that," Kim went on, "but you never killed him. He was knocked unconscious but fully recovered. All the police wanted to find out was who stole the truck."

As it began to sink in, I asked,

"What about that American youngster on the bus? She told me he was dead."

"Well you know how rumours get exaggerated, and she probably thought it was true."

"But there were roadblocks," I insisted.

"The police were trying to find the culprit, and you thought you were on the run, and probably imagined every situation was being directed at you."

She was right. I was convinced that I was being hunted for the soldier's death and saw danger in every situation that was probably quite normal. As my mind went back over it, I remembered the waitress in Brig, disappointed at my hasty departure.

Kim was speaking again.

"Now you know the truth you can drive to Switzerland with nothing to fear, but I will have blown the whole operation. What will happen to me I don't know, I've disobeyed orders but at least I've levelled with you, and I'm glad I've told you."

Sitting there in the darkness, I realised how much the thought of the soldier had troubled me. There had been times that I'd forgotten it, but it always returned.

We both said nothing for a moment, then she went on,

"Now that I've told you everything, I'm asking you to help me a bit longer, and drive me back so I can carry out my instructions."

Squeezing her hand, I didn't hesitate before answering.

"I need my bloody head examined, but you win."

Reaching over, I found her shoulders and drew her across, feeling her body soften as she came towards me. Our lips met in soft open contact that roused a thrill in me, and that triggered thoughts of what might be to come.

"Thanks ski-man," she said, "I knew I could count on you."

As the moment passed, I came back to the present, and flicking on the interior light I turned to see how Helen was. She was curled up on the seat, obviously in an exhausted sleep.

Turning back, I was about to flick off the light when a thought struck me.

"What if I'd refused?" I asked.

"I still have the gun," she said.

"Well supposing you'd threatened me, and I still refused to turn back?"

"Then I'd have used it," she said quietly.

I looked at her in the dim light.

"Beautiful," I said.

She smiled.

"I was only joking, Matt," she said. "Come on, we haven't got much time."

"I'm glad to hear it," I said, "it would make me nervous in bed — spiders kill their mates you know."

We both laughed, and I swung the Alfa around and headed back towards the villa. I wondered what might lie ahead, and I had an uneasy feeling that she had meant it.

Chapter 13

The knowledge that the soldier was okay gave me a terrific lift. I knew that heading back would almost certainly mean we would encounter the others again, but it didn't worry me. In fact, the thought excited me as I drove the little car back along the road. I'd overcome the fatigue barrier, but it had left me a little lightheaded, failing to realise the full consequences of my action. It wasn't long before reality caught up with me again.

We had passed the villa and were two or three miles along the coast road, when I spotted two cars ahead of us. One was on our side, and the other was facing us on the other side of the road. By the overhead lighting I could see them outside talking to each other. Dropping down a cog, I gave the engine full blast and headed straight for the gap between the two cars.

"Here we go!" I shouted as Kim braced herself against the fascia.

"Look out, Matt — you won't make it!" she yelled.

It was too late to change my mind, and we hurtled forwards towards the alarmingly small gap between the two vehicles. The Italians scattered, and with an ear-splitting crash we cannoned through.

"Holy shit!" Kim panted, "That was close."

The Alfa was still handling okay, but it had suffered more damage to the side where the headlight was already broken.

As she looked back, she said,

"There's only one following us, you must have busted the other one."

I was struggling to see ahead well enough to pull away from them, and then I felt an increasing amount of wheel shake transmitted through the steering.

"How far do we have to go?" I asked hastily.

"I can't be sure," she replied, "but I must get to a phone as soon as we shake them off."

I was beginning to have second thoughts about tangling with the Italians again.

"That won't be easy, they're gaining on us; I'll have to try and turn off somewhere and hope we can lose them."

The Alfa needed all my skill to keep it on the road. Every bend was a problem as the steering got progressively sloppy and wouldn't take much more punishment from fast cornering.

Rounding the next bend, I suddenly saw the flashing red lights of a slowly descending barrier.

Continental railway crossings are notorious for their short warnings, before dropping the barricade across, in front of oncoming traffic. This one was no exception and I accelerated forwards. We shot under the first pole, and just made it under the second, before Kim realised what was happening.

"Look out!" she cried, but we were already through.

I heard the squeal of tyres as our pursuer tried to stop, followed by a crescendo of breaking glass and tearing metal.

"Quick, pull over!" Kim shouted, and almost before we stopped, she was out and running back.

As I joined her, I could see that the poles had ripped off the top of the car and it had left the road and hit a tree. It was on its side with the wheels still spinning. In the lights from the crossing I could see two mangled bodies inside, and on the other side another body was on the ground. As I bent to examine it, I turned it over and saw the lifeless face of Garlic Mouth.

Looking down I felt nothing. No revengeful pleasure at his death, no remorse at seeing his battered lifeless body, nothing. Our encounter was over, and I had won, but it all seemed so unreal there was no feeling of emotion about it. This is how it must be in war, I thought, you merely kill the other fellow and then turn away and go on living.

His coat was open, and I felt in the pockets. I pulled out a lumpy object and held it to the light.

"Well I'm buggered!" I exclaimed. "I never expected to see you again."

It was my old pistol. Dropping it into my pocket, it seemed a long time ago that I had purchased it from the queer old woman in Visp.

A goods train clanged past, its driver unaware of the accident, and as it rumbled away, an old man from the crossing house came towards us, calling out in Italian.

"I'll see him," Kim said. "There's bound to be a phone I can use." With that she made off, leaving me by the wreck. She came back a few minutes later and began to tell me of her phone call.

"The plan's been changed," she said. "I must take Helen to Milan, to the Hotel Europa, and my contact will meet us there. Can you nurse the car that far?"

I indicated towards the wreckage. "What about this lot?" I asked her.

"To hell with it! The old man's calling the police and when they arrive, we'll be long gone."

"Suits me," I said. "The sooner we get to Milan the better. If I take it easy, we should make it."

Kim laughed, and taking my arm we walked along the road towards the Alfa.

"If you get us there, we'll deliver Helen and then celebrate." She looked up into my face as she spoke, then kissing my cheek, she whispered, "Together."

My feelings were aroused again at the thought of that togetherness.

She made Helen comfortable, although her condition still concerned me. The steering behaved erratically, but at a more sedate speed gave me little trouble. It was pretty late when we reached Milan and found the hotel.

It was a large modern establishment, and the night staff were expecting our arrival. There was a message for Kim to say that we should stay the night and would be contacted in the morning.

Kim took Helen to get washed up, and I asked the porter to move the car to the hotel garage. I just had time to freshen up before Kim joined me again and beckoned me to the restaurant.

"Helen's asleep," she said.

"Good, I hope she feels better by the morning."

We sat down.

"They're bringing us something from the kitchen," she said. "I sure feel ready for it."

"Me too — what about a drink, do you think they can rustle up a bottle at this time of night?"

"I hope so," she replied, "the waiter said he'd do his best."

The meal came and we tucked in. It was a variety of cold meats with mixed salad, and halfway through the waiter arrived with a litre of Valpolicelli.

We finished the meal and Kim got up.

"I'll shake down in Helen's room, there's two beds there. They've given you another room further along the corridor," she said.

"What about our celebration together — remember?" I asked.

"It's too late now, Matt, and I've lost the mood. Let's make it tomorrow night — okay?"

"Okay," I replied, "but make sure you bolt your door in case I walk in my sleep."

She left, and I stayed on and finished the bottle. Twenty minutes later I found my room and turned in. I wasn't sorry to be sleeping alone and didn't need any rocking.

Next morning, I joined the two of them at breakfast, and Helen had returned to something approaching normality. She didn't say much but took some food and coffee and began to look better.

"Any news?" I asked.

"Yes, we'll be met later and we're to wait here till they come."

"Then what?"

"Helen will be taken to a private clinic for a check-up, and her father will be informed of her safety."

I looked at Helen, waiting for her to say something, but she remained silent, so I turned back to Kim.

"What about you — us?" I asked.

"I'm not sure yet. I guess I'll be free for a bit, I'll know more when they arrive."

I left it at that. It was no use pushing it, as nothing could be done until Helen was off our hands.

"These ski boots are killing me," I said. "If you don't need me, I'll go shopping and treat myself to some Italian shoes."

"Sure, go ahead, there should be plenty of time before the others get here."

"What about you and Helen? I'm sure you would both like some clean clothes."

"We can't leave, but it's being taken care of, the others are bringing it."

"Mother dear, you think of everything." I gibed.

She grinned, but I wasn't sure that she was amused.

I left the hotel and made my way to the garage in the morning sun. I thought that I'd take a look at the car in daylight, but it wasn't there. I thought that Kim had probably arranged for it to be repaired, so I made off for the shops on foot. Enjoying my new- found freedom, I ambled along content to take in the sights. I stopped several times to look into shop windows, then got the feeling I was being followed. It must be my imagination, I told myself; I was getting too melodramatic since my involvement in this affair.

I continued window shopping, crossing the street several times, but wherever I went it wasn't long before a guy in a grey suit showed up behind me. When I glanced back, he would stop and look in a window. I couldn't distinguish his features, but he was rather stout, around fifty, with silvery hair and wore an open sheepskin jacket over his suit.

Coming to a shoe shop, I went in and waited for the assistant. Looking back, I saw my tail pass outside without so much as a glance through the window. Was I was being stupid? He was just looking at the shops and was probably curious about me because I looked like some kind of nut, clomping around the fashion shops of Milan in ski boots.

The shoes wouldn't be practical, so I selected a pair of zip-up sealskin boots. The assistant watched, as I zipped them up and I gave him my old boots, indicating for him to dump them.

I paid with the lira I had taken from John Wallace and left to continue shopping.

Back at the hotel, I went to my room then along to Kim and Helen. I knocked a couple of times but there was no response. I began to feel a little uneasy but descending to the lounge this feeling was short-lived. Kim was sitting there with three others, two men and a girl. They all looked rather young and student-like. When she saw me, she left them and came across to me.

"I won't be long, Matt, there's just a couple of things to clear up, and I'll be with you," she said. She looked beautiful and my heart missed a beat as she came close.

"Where's Helen?" I asked.

Kim smiled. "Oh, she's alright, she's gone to the clinic."

Before I could say any more, she left me and re-joined the others.

They weren't interested in me, and my part in the operation was over. My thoughts were now of getting back to Zermatt and spending a few days there with Kim. It wouldn't be worth going on to Riederalp, but the thought of a few days together in Zermatt raised my blood pressure. It wouldn't be relaxing, but what I had in mind was the kind of exhaustion I could look forward to with joyful anticipation.

Kim finished talking to the others, and as they left, she came over to me.

"It's all arranged, we can take the train from here to

Brig and then on to Zermatt. I have to collect my things there, and then go on to Geneva to meet Professor Linstead," she said."

"What for? Can't your Geneva people handle it now?" I asked.

"Well, they think it best if I see him and explain first-hand what's happened." Her voice was soft and persuasive. "I have to see this through, Matt."

I followed her across to a corner table, situated beneath an enormous plant, which covered the wall in a tangled mass of leaves and aerial roots that hung over the archway. We sat down and looked at each other across the table.

"How long will it take?" I asked her. "Can't we both go to Geneva? And then when you've seen him, we could go back to Zermatt and have some time alone together."

"No, that's not possible."

"I don't see why," I persisted. "What's to stop us?"

"Well you don't seem to understand, Matt, I'm not like you, I have to obey orders and I'm wanted for another assignment."

"Tell them to stuff their orders," I said angrily. "We've got some unwinding to do together — remember?"

She smiled at me, and even after the past few days still managed to look lovely. It had been hectic, and often frighteningly dangerous, but there wasn't a trace of it in her face. She leaned forwards towards me. "It'll be fine, Matt, I haven't forgotten, I shall stay on in Zermatt overnight."

"Overnight!" I complained. "I figured we'd have at least a few days together."

Thoughts of having her to myself had been tantalising my imagination, since we kissed in the car before the chase. The thought of holding her, caressing her, and making love had aroused a passion within me like nothing I'd felt before. I wanted her, needed her, needed to share the zest for life that she aroused within me. As for the future I didn't give a damn. What mattered now was today, and each single day that followed, enjoying them as they came, with no thought of the day before or the one after.

Kim was laughing as she found my hand across the table and held it firmly.

"The way I'll unwind you tonight, you won't be fit for anything for a few days," she said wickedly, tweaking my nose between the thumb and forefinger of her free hand.

I laughed with her, catching the infectiousness of her mood.

"I'll make sure to take plenty of vitamins today, so I don't disappoint you," I retorted, removing her hand from my nose and pressing my thumb into her palm.

"Better make that oysters," she said.

A waiter came over and asked if we wanted anything, but being close to lunch, we decided to go to our rooms and freshen up and meet back down in the restaurant later. There was a train from Milan Central that would get us to Brig in time for the connection to Zermatt, and we'd be there in time for the evening. Remembering, I asked,

"What happened about the car? It's not in the garage."

She hesitated momentarily.

"Err — I had it taken to a repair depot. I figured it would be safer than leaving it here to attract attention. They came and took it before breakfast."

I nodded. It didn't matter now what happened to it.

"What about Helen, will she be staying on at the clinic?"

"Only until she's fit enough to travel, then as soon as I've seen the professor, we'll fly her to Geneva to join him. If all goes well, they'll both be in the States in a few days."

It occurred to me that after he was reunited with his daughter, the professor might want to stay in Switzerland, but I didn't pursue the point. It would be a problem for them to worry about. My only worry was that something might happen that prevented us from reaching Zermatt by this evening.

We reached my room and standing with her by the door was intoxicating. The thought of sharing a bed with her, with nothing more dangerous than the possibility of it collapsing beneath us, caused my hormones to get rampant and swell my ego.

"Would you like to come in?" I asked.

"Not now," she answered, so I gave her a playful dig, and nipped inside before she could retaliate.

"See you at lunch then," I called through the door.

"I'll get you for that later, ski balls," she shouted back.

Chapter 14

She looked great when I met her for lunch, wearing a turquoise cashmere jumper, and with the tints in her hair gleaming from the newness of a salon hairdo.

"Where would madam care to sit?" I asked her, bowing mockingly, and enacting royal protocol.

"Cut the crap and take me through," she said quietly. "Do you want everyone looking at us?"

"I don't give a damn if they do," I replied. "I'm enjoying myself and I don't care if it shows."

Kim giggled.

"I guess I don't give a hang either," she said. "Come on let's go in."

As the waiter led us to our table, I asked her where she obtained the sweater and the hairdo.

"There's a beauty salon and boutique here in the hotel so I thought I'd make use of it. That's why I'm a little late," she said.

We took our seats and looked across at each other.

"It was worth the wait," I said. "I wish that I looked more elegant."

It was her turn to poke fun.

"You look just dandy ski-man," she drawled, in a mock accent of the Deep South. "At least you've managed to shave."

"Yes, the hotel thinks of everything you might need in the room," I answered.

We settled down to study the menu. The meal wasn't particularly inspiring, but then the plushness of these grand establishments is sometimes unmatched by the output from their kitchens. It was passable enough and in any case my mind wasn't really on the food, as I was watching the clock for fear that we would linger over it and miss the train. Whatever happened, I was determined that we got to Zermatt to enjoy this evening.

We finished the meal and leaving Kim to settle our bills and order a taxi to take us to the station, I went up to my room. Our train left at 13.40 so we had agreed to meet back in the lobby at twenty past which would allow the taxi enough time to get us there.

I went down a little early, and she wasn't there so I hung around idly passing the time. Walking over to the glass-fronted show cases that the local craftsmen use to demonstrate their wares, I began glancing over them. Five minutes passed, then ten, and I began to get edgy. Going to the desk, I enquired if Miss Summers had paid our bill and ordered a taxi. The girl at the desk didn't speak English, and I didn't know much Italian, so she finished up sending for the manager. By the time he arrived Kim still hadn't come, and I knew that we'd be too late for the train. He explained that the bill had been paid and he thought Miss Summers had gone off in the taxi.

I couldn't understand how or why this had happened, but there was nothing I could do about it now.

The manager looked up the next train to Brig, and there was one at fifteen hundred, so I ordered a taxi for two thirty and went back to my room.

"Bloody hell!" I fumed, and slamming the door I leaped across the bed, using it as a trampoline and landed by the wardrobe. Giving it a resounding thump with the flat of my hand, I swore loudly again to relieve my agitation. It frightened the life out of the poor chambermaid, who was changing the towels in the bathroom. Giving a shriek, she fled hurriedly across the bedroom and disappeared through the door, jabbering her apologies at the shock of my rapid intrusion.

The hour that I had to wait dragged until it was time to depart. Leaving a tip for the chambermaid, by way of an apology for her fright, I left and made my way to the hotel entrance as the taxi drew up outside. I wanted to ask if he was the same one that Kim had used earlier, but it was useless because of the language barrier.

The traffic in Milan is as bad as you'll find anywhere. In the city centre, five lanes of traffic merge and cross in all directions, with no one giving way until a split second before a crash is imminent. The whole manoeuvre is carried out at breakneck speed, with much honking of horns, shouted abuse and two finger gestures, in reply to the shaken fists. Italian drivers are the most impatient in the world, and when we had to wait at the traffic lights on red, it proved too much for the driver of a low sports car in the next lane. Seeing a filter showing green, he drove over the central obstacle at high speed, leaving his exhaust on the raised edge of the island. I thought there must be a high rate of heart attacks in the city, due to the permanently raised blood pressure of its inhabitants.

We reached the station unscathed and in good time. I paid the driver from my bundle of lira and gave him a hefty tip to help compensate for his inevitably shortened life span.

Buying my ticket, I mingled with the crowd that were waiting. The train arrived, snaking into the station with the loudspeakers announcing its arrival and destination.

I wondered if Kim would be waiting for me at Brig, or perhaps she'd go on to Zermatt and catch up with me later. The fact that my ambitions would be thwarted if she wasn't there angered me. Then a nagging thought about her safety began troubling me. I couldn't think of anything that would endanger her safety, now we had got rid of Helen's kidnappers, as there was nothing to link us to their deaths. There were probably KGB agents in the area, but I couldn't see how they could be onto us yet. Nevertheless, Kim had gone without a word and I was at a loss for an explanation.

I was still thinking about it as I boarded the train and sat in a window seat opposite an elderly couple, who glanced at me and then returned to the books they were reading.

There was another possibility. I could have been jilted!

The prospect of that didn't please me.

But Kim had been as strong for our night together as I was, and she wouldn't have gone off me that suddenly. No, there had to be another reason.

I glanced out of the window along the platform, as my mind juggled with the alternatives. She had made it clear that she had to obey orders and there could have been a last-minute change. Surely though she would have found a way to let me know.

As the train started to pull away, my attention was caught by the figure of a man running along the platform in an effort to jump on. I couldn't see him properly but pressing my head to the glass I managed to get a better look at him as he clambered on board. I caught a glimpse of his grey suit, and as he reached for the handrail, I could see the sleeve of a sheepskin coat.

I was sure, well almost sure, that it was the same man that I had spotted following me earlier.

It would be too much of a coincidence for him to just happen to be going to Brig. It didn't make sense. Could he be working for a rival organisation that was monitoring our movements?

Then I remembered that at our first meeting, Kim had been suspicious that I was with the KGB.

Now I started to feel vulnerable again. I had thought it was all over except for the pay-off night with Kim, now I could be involved again with Christ knows what to come, and I cursed at the thought.

If he was out to find Helen, he could be trailing me as his link to her, and Kim could have known and made off without contacting me.

Reaching into my pocket, I felt the gun and sat clutching it as I considered what to do next. I was safe enough on the train, but the trouble would be when we reached Brig. Assuming he had only picked up my trail in Milan, if I could dodge him in Brig, I would have the advantage, as he wouldn't know where I was going. I would then have to find a way to take the train to Zermatt without him knowing.

The Italian countryside flashed past as I kept a watchful eye on the passengers that came along the central walkway. My man didn't appear, but he would be watching me from further along the train when we arrived. It seemed to take a long time before we approached the border at Iselle, and when we did arrive there was a delay for passport and ticket checks. It also shunted about to pick up the wagons with the vehicles and passengers en route to Switzerland through the Simplon tunnel. My estimated time of arrival was going to be wrong, as it was already getting close to dusk and there was a long journey ahead through the tunnel, and it would be getting dark when we reached Brig.

With the attachments made, the train pulled away from the sidings and began its climb towards the tunnel. Progress was slow with the extra weight and the rising gradient. I was in a forward carriage facing the rear, so

I didn't see the tunnel entrance as we entered. Suddenly we were plunged into darkness with a tremendous increase in noise, as the sound hit the tunnel sides and echoed back into the carriage. I gripped the pistol in alarm at the total blackness and crescendo of noise. Then the carriage flooded with light as the engineer switched on the generator. After some time, we emerged from the tunnel into the fading daylight and quickly completed the remaining distance to Brig.

As the platform came into view, I rose from my seat and made for the door. My plan was to jump out quickly and shake him off. I wasn't familiar with entering Brig from this direction, and soon realised that the front of the train where I stood was being taken through the station to the far end of the platform so that the cars could drive off. It meant that the station exit would be at the other end of the carriages.

I mingled with the alighting passengers and hurried along, keeping a watchful eye to spot him first. Halfway along I spotted him. He was still on the train, standing back in the doorway, leaning on the partition. I reached the exit into the main hall and paused at a kiosk. Looking down at the newspapers, I selected a day-old Financial Times. Paying for it, I glanced back and saw matey in the main assembly area. I turned and walked to the middle of the lobby, unfolding the paper as I went. He had carried on through to the street outside.

Was I mistaken about him, or would he be furtively watching for me from outside?

I needed to go that way for the Zermatt train, without tipping him off as to my destination. Holding the newspaper in front of me, and pretending to read it, I looked over the top to the timetable posters on the wall. Spotting the one I needed, I walked towards it pretending to be engrossed in the newspaper. The last train to Zermatt left at 18.44.

I lowered the paper and walked towards the door. Now would be the test.

Out on the street, I spotted him standing by the row of taxis parked along the kerb. Too late to do anything else, I walked straight past him, crossed the street, and made off into the town. As I walked briskly through the shopping centre, the streetlights were glowing red as they warmed up in the cold twilight. Mingling with the shoppers, I hoped that I was worrying for nothing, but looking back confirmed that I hadn't been. He was further back, but I had no doubt that he was following me.

I would have to lose him quickly and then double back through the side streets to get to my train. I threw the newspaper into a rubbish bin, and saw he was still there. I knew the town and the next turning was the last one that took me towards my train, but if I took it, he would know where I was heading.

"All right then, matey — I'll try something else," I muttered to myself, as an idea struck me.

Coming to the bridge spanning the Rhone, I crossed and went up the stone steps into the Eggishorn Hotel.

The tables were empty, and I chose one by the counter facing the door. Someone came through from the kitchen behind me and came to my table. Looking up, I saw it was Titsalina, and the buttons of her blouse were still struggling to hang on. Every breath she took held my attention, as each of her nipples forced out their impression on the flimsy material. The magnificent two had faded from my memory but seeing them for real once more renewed my desire.

"Tea citron, bitte," I said, smiling at her.

She nodded and turned away, not recognising me at first, but then hesitated and turned back.

"Hello again," I said in English.

She looked bemused. "What happened to you before?" she asked.

"Well — yes — I'm afraid I owe you an apology, you see I had to leave in a hurry as something important came up."

She didn't look convinced, so I continued,

"I'm sorry if I caused you any inconvenience."

"Madame wondered what had happened to you, she thought you were unsatisfied — with the room," she added.

"No, nothing like that," I said, "It's just that I had to go somewhere."

"Will you be wanting a room tonight?" She leaned forwards against the edge of the table as she spoke, causing her skirt to pull tight across her thighs, outlining the V in the middle where they met the table.

My mind raced as I considered the alternatives. I could stay here and be sure, well practically sure, of a night with Titsalina, or I could get back to Zermatt on the hope of finding Kim.

A bird in the hand is worth two in the bush, I thought, and my hands were itching to get onto this bird.

It was tempting, but I wouldn't rest until I knew that Kim was safe, and besides there was still matey outside.

"No, not tonight," I said, "but I'll probably be back in a few days."

"Oh, that's good — I know you'll like it here," she said and went off to fetch my tea.

I went over to the door and peered out. Sure enough, matey was standing at the entrance to the car park. I looked at the time and there was only seven minutes to the train. I went across to the stairs, and taking them two at a time, I reached the top and turned along the landing. There was a door at the end leading down to the street, and seconds later I was skirting the hotel and hurrying to the train. I paused to look back and felt sure I had given him the slip.

The Zermatt train was waiting. I climbed the iron steps into the carriage and looked back.

Still no sign of him. I took a seat and looked at the time. A minute later the train gave a jolt and began rolling slowly away, creaking and groaning as it crossed the points across the road, and began the journey to Zermatt.

I breathed a sigh of relief and settled back for the

journey. Now if Kim were there everything would have been perfect.

Then my heart sank as the connecting door opened and matey entered and sat down. As he did our eyes met, and I knew that he knew I was wise to him.

He couldn't have seen me leave the hotel. I was sure of that. He must have gone in and discovered that I'd gone, and then made his way here assuming I'd taken the train. It didn't matter now; he was here and would stick close to me until he saw an opportunity to move in. It must be to do with Helen; maybe he was KGB, but it would dash my hopes of a night with Kim.

The train continued to Visp to pick up more passengers, and I remained seated as other passengers began getting off. As others began getting on, I jumped up and dived through to the intersection. I leaped out of the open door and ran along the platform to the toilets. Stopping to look back he was in hot pursuit. I gave the 'Herren' swing door a hefty push, then I ran around the corner as it closed with a resounding crash. Not waiting to see if my ruse had worked, I dived into the 'Damen' door.

An old lady stood there with her dress up, making some adjustments to her underclothes. She looked at me in terror and opened her mouth to scream. Giving her a big smile, I pressed my finger to my nose, pursed my lips, and let out a loud 'shush' as I winked at her. She closed her mouth and stood there petrified. Turning back, I peered out and saw the train gathering speed along the platform. Waiting for the last coach to get level with me, I looked back and saw the old girl gaping at me. She was so mesmerised she had forgotten to drop her dress and was still holding it up, with the tops of her stockings and old black garters in full view.

I blew her a kiss and sprinted for the train. For a moment I thought that I wouldn't make it, but I hammered my legs along in a final spurt, and felt my fingers catch the upright handrail of the last door. Leaping onto the bottom step, I clung to the handle and looked back.

Matey was pulling up, having lost his puff.

I leaned out, making sure he could see me, as I waved him a 'Harvey Smith' at arm's length.

"Up yours, matey!" I shouted to him gleefully.

He could do what he liked now, but he couldn't get to Zermatt until the morning. And tonight, was mine.

Chapter 15

There was one stop on the way up the valley, at the little halt of St. Niklaus. There was a road from Visp to here, but it was very winding, and matey could never make it in time to beat the train and take it for the final distance to Zermatt. As we pulled away from the halt, my thoughts turned to Kim's disappearance in Milan. I felt excitement at the thought of a night with her, but at the same time there was a gnawing uneasiness that she wouldn't be there. Maybe she'd only played me along 'till the job was done, and now she'd skipped and left me flat.

"Could be," I muttered to myself, in answer to my thoughts. Then, trying to convince myself that my doubts were unfounded, "No, she'll be there alright," I said.

In any case I could go back to Brig, and there was always Titsalina. But that might prove difficult as by now she would be thinking that I was some kind of a nut, and there would still be matey to contend with.

My mind was still stewing things over when we arrived at Zermatt. There were no horse taxis outside, so I made my way on foot towards the Grand Hotel. The doorman gave me his usual salute as he opened the door for me to enter. Going through to the reception desk, I rang the bell and waited. Coming from his office, the duty manager recognised me and greeted me by name.

"Your room is ready for you, Mr Sands," he said, giving me the key, "and Miss Summers left word to say that she would like to see you as soon as you arrived."

"Oh, she got here then." I tried not to sound surprised but blurted it out before I had time to check myself. "Thanks, I'll go up straight away."

As I walked away, he called after me. "Miss Summers has changed her room — she's now in the room next to yours." I thought that he had just the slightest grin on his face as he told me.

Wasting no time getting to my room, I threw off my anorak as I crossed to the connecting door.

It was locked, so I knocked and called, "Kim, are you there?"

A noise came from the other side, then the door opened, and she stood there dressed in the same outfit that she'd worn the first time we met.

About to say something nice, instead I asked sharply,

"What the bloody hell happened to you in Milan?"

She looked at me in silence. Then realising that my outburst was more in relief than in anger, she stepped forwards, and placing her hands on my shoulders, she kissed me. Then she walked silently back into her room, and I followed her and sat down on the corner of the bed.

"Well, what happened?" I asked gently.

"I'm sorry about the foul-up, Matt, but when I went to arrange for the car to be collected, the repairs took longer than I expected. I realised that I couldn't get back in time to meet you, so I dashed to the station as the train was about to leave." I nodded and she went on.

"Well I just made it and was expecting to find you already on board. When you weren't I couldn't do anything until it got to the next station, so then I phoned the hotel and they said you'd left. I figured that you'd be following on the next train."

"You figured right," I said, and was about to tell her about my trip, but she went on.

"I thought it best to come on ahead and fix up for our rooms here tonight." She smiled at me and I returned her smile but said nothing. I thought it best not to tell her about matey, in case it resulted in her changing her mind about tonight and dashing off to report it to her contacts.

"Well, all's well that ends well," I said, "but you had me worried for a while."

"Worried?" She raised her eyebrows. "Did you think I'd run out on you?"

I lay back on the bed, raising my hands and placing them behind my head.

"The thought did occur to me," I said, "until I remembered the uncontrollable urge you have for me."

I wasn't quite ready for the weight of her, as she threw herself on me, causing me to gasp.

"You conceited old goat," she said, laughing, "I

could find a dozen young guys in Zermatt that could outstay you and satisfy a girl's needs — no matter what she wanted."

"Correction," I said, "The youngsters haven't got the staying power. I'm improving like good wine, remember?"

"That so?" she said. "We'll see about that!" Pulling at my shirt and running her hands inside, she said, "Let's see if I can fizz you up, and make your cork pop."

I began laughing as she tickled me, and we rolled over together across the bed and onto the floor. Although it was fun, my body was still feeling the effect of the last few days.

"Hey, let's save the horse play for later." I giggled.

We stopped, and lay with our arms entwined, on the floor beside the bed.

"What say I get cleaned up and we have a drink before dinner?" I suggested.

"Good idea, ski-man, but don't take too long, I'm sure hungry." Then she added, pushing my hand away from the inside of her thigh, "For food." Giving me a dig in the ribs, she got to her feet.

"I'll take a bath and change, and then we'll go down for that drink — I won't be long," I told her.

"Shall we eat here, Matt, or go out somewhere?" she called to me.

"I don't care," I called back. "Let's see how we feel after our aperitif."

She didn't bother to close the connecting door, and

I could hear her singing as I ran the water. It felt good to let the hot water soak into my skin, and it greatly relieved the soreness of my body.

Kim carried on the conversation through the open door, as I got dressed. I was buttoning my shirt front as she came through carrying a programme.

"It says here that there's a folklore soiree on tonight — what's that, Matt?"

I finished buttoning my shirt.

"It's an evening of dancing and local pageantry. A kind of Swiss country and western."

"That sounds like fun," she said, "shall we go?"

"Where is it?"

"It says it's at the Hotel Alpenrose."

"The Alpenrose?"

"Yeh."

"That's some way from here, but I don't mind, if you'd like to go."

She looked pleased.

"It says there's a restaurant so we could eat there — make it a kind of celebration," she said.

"Okay, but how are we going to get there?"

"It can't be that far, Matt, and it's a lovely night, why don't we just walk?"

"I thought I'd finished with hiking," I said, but seeing her enthusiasm, I told her, "Okay — if you want to."

"It'll be great"," she said.

We collected our personal items and prepared to

leave. She seemed happy, and at her girlish best.

"I'll lock my door from inside and come out with you," she said, "then we'll only need to take one key."

On the way out, I checked the way there with the night clerk, as I deposited my key. The temperature had dropped rapidly; the thermometer at the end of the hotel drive showed it was minus seven.

We linked arms and walked briskly along the pavement, the snow squeaking as we crunched along.

It was a beautiful starlit night, and the Matterhorn looked so close that I felt that I could reach up and touch it, as it stood silhouetted against the deep purple sky.

Kim cuddled in closer and looked up into my face. "Gee, Matt, I feel so happy now, I'd almost forgotten how romantic it can be on nights like this."

I squeezed her arm with mine.

"It's the stuff dreams are made of," I said. "For those lucky enough to enjoy them, it's these magic moments that are the highlights that make up a lifetime. The chap who wrote that song for Perry Como knew exactly how it was."

We continued walking along and she continued looking up at me.

"You could turn a girl's head with talk like that," she said. "I never realised you were such a romantic. I took you for the hard-boiled type."

"You should never judge an egg by its shell," I said.

The breath from our conversation made vapour trails, as we continued along.

A horse-drawn sleigh came jingling towards us, kicking up little chunks of hard packed snow as we stood beneath a lamp waiting for it to pass. It was like a scene from Doctor Zhivago, as the horse went trotting by, its nostrils blowing out clouds of steam from the effort, as the driver in his big fur coat sat flicking his long whip. He was dressed for the cold, complete with a fur hat and long, shaggy fur boots. Kim gave a wave to the two blanketed passengers as they glided past. The jingling of the harness carried through the clear night air long after they were out of sight.

"Oh, Matt, this is so beautiful, why can't life be like this all the time?" she said whimsically.

"Maybe we wouldn't appreciate these magic moments if it was. The important thing is to be sure to recognise them when they come and store them in your memory for your old age."

"Kiss me," she whispered.

We kissed beneath the streetlight and stood enjoying the moment. Pushing her away, I said, "Come on, let's find that hotel — I'm bloody starved."

"Men!" she exclaimed. "I was right the first time. You're about as romantic as a…" she paused, lost for the word she wanted, "as a…" she repeated.

"As a hungry lover," I told her. "Love and full stomachs go together."

"Like hell they do!" she retorted. "Haven't you heard of the lean and hungry look?"

"That's for the very young," I retorted, "but you're

hooked on the vintage stuff now, remember? Besides, I thought you were hungry just now."

She laughed,

"That's right, I am — come on."

Ten minutes later we came to the hotel, where under the overhanging roof was a large signboard that read 'Hotel Alpenrose Folklore Soiree Heute Abend' The menus, on the board lower down, showed that there were two set menus as well as the a la carte.

Pushing open the door, we joined the lively crowd inside and made our way towards the tables. A waiter met us and led us to a table for two, which was the only one free. He gave us the menu cards and left. It was very noisy and not the sort of thing that I'd planned for this evening, but Kim seemed to be enjoying it, so I didn't say anything to spoil it for her. It was clear that most of the revellers were locals, and it was obviously an event they looked forward to as their big night out.

Kim spoke first.

"Which shall we have? The set menu or the a la carte?"

Taking a look at the set choices, I found they didn't stir my gastric juices, being either pork cutlets or veal fritters.

"Let's try something from the a la carte side," I said, looking across to see her reaction.

"Okay," she said, "what about the fondue Bourguignonne?"

"Yes, that's fine. I'll try to catch the waiter's eye

and order now, as it's bound to take some time to set up, with all this hubbub going on."

It took several minutes before a waiter came within hailing distance, but to his credit he came as soon as he'd finished at a nearby table and took our order.

As he hurried away, three men dressed in Swiss costumes came onto the small stage at the end of the dining room. Without a microphone, the leader spoke to the audience.

"Mein damen und herren," he began, following this with the evening's programme.

As it was spoken in a Swiss-Deutsch dialect, I could understand the gist of it, and explained to Kim what we were in for.

"There'll be music and dancing, and a yodelling group, and I think after that some local group will perform a play or something."

"Sounds like fun," she said, her face flushed with excitement. "I'm enjoying this, aren't you?"

"It's great," I replied, hoping I sounded more convincing than I felt. "I hope it doesn't go on too long though."

"Well our time's our own now, so let's enjoy ourselves," she said.

People began dancing to the trio, and there was no sign of our meal, so I reached over and asked her if she would like to try it. It was only some sort of two-three hop, and we soon picked up the rhythm.

It meant holding her close, to guide her around the

little space. Feeling her this near made me lose concentration, with the result that we had several collisions, especially with a great oaf in size fourteen boots, after which he would look down from his six feet seven and babble his apologies. After he'd almost winded me for the umpteenth time, I persuaded Kim we'd best sit the rest out. The group continued playing for another fifteen minutes, after which our fondue arrived. We drank a bottle of Dole with the meal, and it lasted through the yodelling, and most of the dramatic performance that followed.

After that, things quietened down, and we sat finishing the wine.

We both began to speak at the same time.

"You first." I said.

"Well, I was going to ask you what you do in England. Do you realise that after all we've been through together in the last few days, I know absolutely nothing about you?"

"I'm in what you'd call the real estate business," I said, "but I've got other plans — do you like horses?"

"Yes, sure, I adore them in fact," she replied.

"Well I'm looking for a place in the country, nothing grand, but big enough for a few horses, where I can ride out into the hills every day and hardly meet a soul."

"Sounds wonderful," she said. "It's the kind of thing we all dream about in our quieter moments."

"It's not just a dream," I told her earnestly. "It's

there waiting to be grabbed, and I'm asking you if you will come and share it with me." Before she could reply I went on. "Look, I'm not asking you to make an irreversible decision, if it doesn't work out, well, okay. But let's try, it could be a lot of fun, and who knows, we might settle down and become a real Darby and Joan in twenty or thirty years."

She smiled at me, and for a moment I thought she was about to agree. Then she leaned forwards, took up her glass, and holding it against her face, she rolled the rim around her chin as she thought.

Finally, she spoke.

"Look Matt, I like you a lot, I think you're a swell guy, and not just because of what's happened. But I have commitments — oh I know that you'll tell me to break them, but it's not that easy."

I began to argue, but she put down the glass then placed her hand on my lips.

"Please, no arguments. Remember what you said about magic moments and storing them up for the future. Well let's make tonight like that. Let's just enjoy each other tonight, and then think about our futures tomorrow in the cold light of dawn."

"I won't argue with that," I said, taking her hand.

There was an announcement from the stage, and an old man stepped forward and began a sort of mournful recitation. I couldn't understand a word, but the rise and fall of his voice was sad, and the faces of those on the other tables reflected this solemnness. Everyone sat

230

quietly except for a group of youngsters, including the village idiot, who, having consumed too much of the local plonk, began making a nuisance of himself. I was about to suggest that we left when I noticed someone coming towards us.

At first, I didn't recognise him, but as he came closer, I saw it was the same guy that Kim had been waiting for the first night we met.

Kim looked surprised. "Kurt! What are you doing here?" she asked him.

He looked at me, then back at her.

"We must talk," he said.

"But how did you know how to find me?"

"I asked at your hotel, and the desk clerk told me you had spoken to him about this place."

Kim turned to me.

"Matt, this is Kurt Van Schmid."

He nodded at me, and I nodded back. I didn't like him, he seemed arrogant, and spoke with a guttural accent that I took to be German.

Kim was speaking.

"But I thought all the arrangements had been made. I'm having fun, can't we talk about it tomorrow?"

I didn't hear his reply, for two things happened simultaneously.

Ignoring the angry shouts from the other tables, the village idiot was trying to perform a handstand on the back of his chair, to the shouted encouragement of his young friends. Pandemonium broke out as other people began shouting at him, as his mates shouted back, while the old man on the stage continued wailing out his tale of woe.

At the same time, I spotted matey coming across the floor towards us. Next came the sound of shattering glass, and I thought a bottle had been knocked over, smashing on the floor beside us. But a fight had broken out between the rival groups of the village youth.

Not waiting, I grabbed Kim and pulled her to her feet, and started pulling her towards the door. Matey saw my move and tried to head us off, but Kurt, who was between us, stepped forwards to intercept him. Seizing the chance, I pushed Kim through the crowd and out through the back door.

Once outside we ran to the corner, crossed the street, and made off along the pavement towards our hotel. Pausing for breath, Kim asked,

"What was that all about?"

"I don't know but let them sort it out."

"Who was that other man, I wonder?" she asked.

"No idea," I lied, "maybe someone took a dislike to Kurt. Do you think he can handle it?"

"Oh yes," she replied, "Kurt can take care of it."

The cold night air filled my lungs, and the alcohol in my blood gave me a heady feeling as I spoke.

"Now let's make it that night to remember, shall we?"

"You're on, ski-man," she said.

As we walked, I wondered how matey had got here.

He must have come up as far as Tasch then somehow made it across country from there. He must have followed Kurt from our hotel to the Alpenrose. Did he have a contact here, who had tipped him off that Kurt was involved, and he decided to follow him? This place must now be crawling with the KGB and CIA, nearly enough to hold a convention I shouldn't wonder, I thought.

Reaching the Grand, I gave the night clerk a hefty tip as I collected my key and told him we weren't to be disturbed. If anyone came looking for us, he was to tell them that we'd checked out.

Taking the fifty-franc note from me, he assured me I could leave it up to him.

I ordered a bottle of Asti to be sent up, and we went up to my room. We had hardly closed the door when a knock came, and a waiter stood there with the wine and glasses. Tipping him, I carried the bottle through to Kim, unwiring the cork as I went. It exploded with a gush of froth, and I realised that I hadn't brought the glasses. Placing my hand over it, I called to Kim to get them, and she quickly obliged.

We laughed and play-acted at linking arms as we drank, and kicking off our boots, sat on the bed propped against the headboard.

"Where will your next assignment be taking you?" I asked her as we drank".

"I don't know — that's probably what Kurt wanted, but let's forget it for tonight."

"I was wondering when I'd see you again," I said seriously. "It's a pity to let it end here."

She kissed my neck and I turned to embrace her. Our lips met in passionate love-play, as I dropped the empty bottle and encircled her shoulders with my arms.

"Come away with me, Kim, come to England with me." I whispered.

"You agreed to discuss it in the morning," she said.

"I know, but I'd like to know now." I stroked her hair and tried to continue, but she interrupted me.

"I know that it's difficult for you to understand," she said softly, "but I vowed that I would never get into a serious relationship again."

I began undressing her as I replied.

"It needn't be like that, we're both adult enough, to enjoy an intimate affair, without it getting too deep."

She took my hand and halted my progress.

"It wouldn't be like that, it would develop into something serious, I can feel that it would. I've gotten to like you an awful lot these past days, in fact I'm beginning to fall in love with you," she whispered.

Her admission stirred my feelings, and I suggested that at least we should arrange to meet after she'd made contact in Geneva and finished this assignment.

"Please drop it, Matt, don't let it spoil our night together," she said.

Resigning myself to her finality and vowing to myself to try again in the morning, I kissed her.

"Okay," I said, "but promise me one thing."

"I can't make any promises, you know that."

"I think you can this one."

"What is it?"

"I shall be returning to England in a few days. If you change your mind when you get to Geneva, will you promise to contact me before I leave?"

"I won't change my mind — I can't."

"But if you do," I persisted, "will you promise to get in touch with me?"

She hesitated, and encouraged by her weakened resolve, I held her tightly and whispered in her ear.

"Promise that you'll do it, if you change your mind."

, "Alright," she said, facing me. "It seems you won't be satisfied until I do, so I promise."

Releasing my hold on her, I spun around off the bed.

"Where you going?" she said. "Hell, you can be infuriating at times."

"I'll be right back. I'm going to get the address where you can contact me."

I found a pen and wrote down the address of my bank in Brig, then went back and handed it to her.

"Keep this, it's my bank in Brig, and I'll be going there before I leave Switzerland."

Taking it, she grabbed my hand and pulled me down on top of her.

"It's time we uncorked that vintage," she murmured.

We kissed again, as I pressed my body against her. She responded, and I began to struggle to undo our clothes.

"Not like this," she murmured, pushing herself out from beneath me, "let's get undressed properly and get into bed."

I rolled over and looked up at her, as she collected up our discarded clothing. Looking down at me she said,

"I've bought something special for this occasion — it's a surprise for you."

"You're all the surprise I want," I said. "Hurry up and come back here."

Avoiding my outstretched hand, she replied,

"I won't be a minute. Do some deep breathing or something."

She disappeared into her room, and I readjusted the pillows and straightened the bed.

"Get undressed while you're waiting for me," she called, through the connecting door. "I fancy you in silk pyjamas."

"I don't have silk pyjamas, it's winceyette or nothing," I called back.

"Boy, you don't believe in fancy labelling for that vintage stuff of yours, do you?" she gibed. "I thought a guy like you would wear something rather more chic." I laughed and retorted.

"When you decant a rare vintage it's best kept warm — if it's chilled, a full- bodied wine loses its flavour. Besides, silk ones always seem to cut me under the arms." I called, "How much longer are you going to be?"

"I'm almost ready," she called back.

I rolled off the bed and finished undressing, and not bothering with pyjamas, I crawled back between the sheets.

"Are you ready?" she called.

"Yes, for Christ's sake, I'm ready."

She appeared in the doorway, and laughing at me, said,

"Who's going t' love you, baby?"

She was naked except for the flimsiest piece of nonsense I'd ever seen. Almost completely transparent, it draped over her shoulders and reached halfway down her thighs. It was held together, well almost held together, with three bows of pink ribbons.

I let out a slow whistle.

"Where'd you get that?"

"In Milan. It's the finest Italian silk. I told the girl in the shop that I wanted the most provocative nightie they had."

"Well it's provoking me alright — come over here."

She turned sideways and I watched her silhouette, outlined by the light from her room, as she reached up the door frame and gyrated her body. The smallness of her waist emphasised the soft roundness of her hips as she wiggled, and I could see the gentle swelling of her lower abdomen and the cupped outline of her firm breasts through the negligee. The fragrance of her body perfume drifted across to me, as she advanced slowly across the room.

Chanting the tune from 'The Stripper', we both

laughed, enjoying the game, as she reached the bottom of the bed and began climbing up towards me. Moments later she was in my arms, and as I gently rolled her over, the nightie fell away, and I caressed the soft pubic hair it revealed. As we kissed and embraced, her hands encompassed me and guided me to her. Making those intimate noises that two people give when they're lost in passion, we reached the point where each of our sexual needs acquired the ultimate fulfilment from each other.

"Hold me tight, Matt — make it last."

"I will, my darling — I will."

The fusion of our naked bodies, violent at first, then softer like the gentle rippling of placid water, gave us the satisfaction that we each sought from each other.

Satisfied, we remained in each other's arms without speaking, just lying there enjoying the warmth and comfort of each other's body.

The unexpected noise of the phone, buzzing in her room, sounded so loud it broke the spell. We both froze and said nothing for several seconds. However, it buzzed away without stopping, and Kim sat up to answer it.

"Sod it! Let it ring," I swore, trying to catch hold of her. She avoided my lunge, and I lay back down, as she stood by the bed. "Come back to bed, it'll stop in a minute," I said.

"Oh hell, I'll have to answer it — it could be important," she said.

She ran through to her bedroom, and I sank back down into the mattress and closed my eyes, letting out a moan. Lying there I could hear her voice from time to time, low and intense, as she answered between periods of listening. I called for her to hang up, but it had no effect.

As I lay there waiting, the softness and warmth of the bed soaked into my body.

It had been a long day, a long week in fact, and I wasn't a kid anymore. It's fine believing that life begins at forty, but a forty-year-old body has its way of showing you it can only take so much punishment. Your physical condition gradually gets left behind and needs time to catch up again. The effect of the warm bed, coupled with the effect of the alcohol, and finally the ultimate satisfaction of making love, was taking its toll.

The soft sheets were caressing me now, and as I stretched out between them, they began lulling me into sleep.

Chapter 16

I gradually came out of my slumber. My mouth was dry, and my head felt muzzy. It was daylight, and everything was quiet, except for some crows that were cawing somewhere in the fir trees outside. I was lying on my right arm, which had gone numb, and rolling over, I expected to see Kim next to me. She wasn't there.

Gathering my thoughts, I stirred to meet the day. I called to Kim, expecting her to answer from her room. Nothing happened, except for the crows that continued their squawking.

Maybe she'd gone to breakfast.

I blinked my eyes in an effort to clear them, and then saw a note on the pillow beside me.

Screwing up my eyes to get them focussed, I read the pencilled message.

'Thanks for your help Ski-man. You were right about the vintage wine. Hope you like the ribbon and it leaves you in the pink — love Kim.'

So, she'd gone.

Well I knew she was off to Geneva today, but I thought that we'd have our last breakfast together.

Maybe it was better this way; at least there were no last-minute goodbyes.

I read the note again. 'Hope you like the ribbon'. I didn't get that part, unless she was referring to the negligee.

Throwing back to covers, I swung my legs over the edge of the bed. Looking down, there was a little pink ribbon tied around my penis. I laughed and pulled one of the loose ends; it came undone. I pulled it off and held it up.

"So that was it," I said. "Well I'm glad she only tied it loosely, or it could have been nasty!"

I was still grinning as I phoned down my order for breakfast and asked for it in my room.

The clerk confirmed that Kim had left early, so I went to the bathroom to prepare myself for the day.

I was feeling better as I dressed and began straightening my things. Then I saw the old pistol, picked it up and balanced it in my hand. Wondering about its history before its experience with me, I realised I never got to fire it.

Going to the window, I opened it and looked across to the fir trees opposite.

"Well why not, it probably won't make much noise," I said. Checking that the magazine was full, I pushed off the safety catch, and aimed at the nearest crow.

There was a click, and nothing happened. On being tried again, it merely clicked once more.

I unloaded it and checked the trigger mechanism. It looked okay but looking closer I could see that the firing pin had been filed off.

"The twisting old cow!" I exclaimed, thinking of the old woman in Visp who had sold it to me. "And to think that my life might have depended on it."

Taking it by the barrel, I threw it at the tree, and falling short, it cartwheeled down and disappeared silently into a bank of snow.

"Well that's that," I said, closing the window. "I wonder if the old girl knew it was useless."

Then I began laughing as it dawned on me. Of course, she did. That was what she was trying to tell me when I bought the ammunition. Oh well, the joke was on me, and I bet when she told her old cronies about the stupid Englishman, they had a good laugh.

I was still chuckling to myself when the waiter came with my breakfast.

"A bloody fine secret service agent you'd be, Sands," I told myself, as I set the tray on the table.

It was a nice day, and I could ski and maybe go back to Brig and find Titsalina. Somehow the prospect of either didn't excite me. I was missing Kim, missing the rapport that had sprung up so naturally between us. Now she had gone, and I would probably never see her again.

What was that old saying? 'Ships that pass in the night'.

I thought of catching the next train to Geneva to try and find her. Then I realised that it wouldn't work. I'd tried my best last night to convince her to stay, but she wouldn't yield.

My thoughts turned to matey, my tail from Milan.

What had happened at the soirée and how did he get there?

Perhaps the news of Helen's kidnap and her reuniting with her father was out. They should be on their way to the States by now and the story was bound to break soon.

Matey would know that he'd missed the boat and there would be no point in his chasing me now. Frankly, I didn't care one way or the other, and I drank the last of the fruit juice and stood up. I would accomplish nothing sitting here; it was time to be moving on.

I had almost finished packing when I heard a knock on the door. Assuming it was the waiter to collect the breakfast tray, I walked across and opened it.

Two men stood outside. The first was tall and athletic looking, about twenty and dressed in ski trousers and fur boots. He wore a striped jersey that emphasised his broad shoulders.

The other man was older, wearing a grey lounge suit. He was of stocky build, beginning to go to fat, but still had the appearance of a man who, when younger, had been a tough physical type.

It was matey.

"Yes?" I asked guardedly.

Matey spoke.

"Mr Sands, I wonder if you could spare us some of your time? There is something we would like to discuss with you."

His voice was soft and pleasant with no hint of

243

menace. His accent was American or possibly Canadian. The Swiss often speak English with an American accent, so maybe he was from the Swiss police. On the other hand, these two could be KGB agents bent on tracking down the professor.

That prospect made me nervous and I thought about what course of action lay open to me if they tried to force their way in.

"What is it you wish to discuss?" I asked.

I was inwardly cursing my stupidity for opening the door and wondered which one I should kick in the balls first if they tried to force their way in.

The younger man was the first to speak.

"Perhaps we should introduce ourselves, my name is Bill Hall, and this is Mr Falconer," he said.

I nodded, and he went on.

"Mr Falconer is with the American delegation to the World Food Organisation based in Geneva. I work for the Office of Multilateral Food Distribution, in the States."

"Nice to meet you," I said and stood there thinking that I'd have a better chance out in the hallway if it came to a punch up.

Seeing my reluctance to retreat inside and allow them access, Falconer reached inside his jacket and I tensed as I thought he was about to draw a gun.

He then produced a wallet. Flipping it open, he held it towards me.

"Here is my identity," he said.

I looked at the photo and official seal. It looked genuine, but these things can be forged.

"I can see that you're not convinced," he went on. "I don't blame you for being careful. Perhaps you would like to ring the World Food Organisation in Geneva. You will find that we do exist and are in the directory."

I didn't answer and stood still, weighing them up.

"Ask to speak to my secretary," he went on, "she will confirm my whereabouts and identity."

If this was a shake down, they would have bundled me inside by now.

"Come in," I said.

I backed away, allowing them to stroll in past me. Falconer made for the phone but I beat him to it.

"I'll make the call," I said and lifting the receiver I dialled the operator.

"I want to place a call to the World Food Organisation in Geneva," I told the girl when she answered. "When you obtain the number, ask to speak to Mr Falconer's secretary. When you're connected ring me back."

The operator spoke English but asked me to repeat the instructions while she took it down.

I then asked for room service and ordered coffee for three to be sent to my room. I didn't need the coffee but wanted someone else here in case this call proved to be a bluff and these cuckoos weren't what they claimed.

Bill Hall advanced towards me.

"You don't believe in taking chances, do you, Mr.

Sands?" he said. Taking out a packet of cigarettes, he offered me one.

"I don't," I said, in answer to both his question and the cigarette. Falconer looked at me.

"When my secretary rings back, I'd like to speak to her if you don't mind."

"I was intending to ask you to," I replied.

The coffee arrived at the same time as the call came through, and I asked the waiter to hang on until I'd taken the call. I asked her about Falconer and his whereabouts, and she agreed to speak to him and then confirm to me that it was him talking.

He took the phone. "Hello, Martina, it's alright, I just need you to confirm my voice. It concerns the investigation, and I need you to establish my identity so that Mr Sands here will help us with some information."

He handed me back the phone. I spoke briefly then hung up. It seemed to be on the level, so I thanked the waiter, and tipping him, said he could leave.

Seating myself at the table, I indicated towards the low modern settee along the wall. They both sat down, and the young American took up the conversation.

"You may have heard of the organisation that I work for in the States."

"Yes," I replied, "don't you monitor US Food aid through the UN? To the underdeveloped countries."

"That's right," he went on, "but not only the underdeveloped countries. All the world food distribution goes through my office, including grain to the USSR."

"That gives you a powerful political weapon," I said. "I believe it's known as 'Agripower' isn't it?"

They looked at each other, then Falconer spoke. "We won't beat about the bush. You seem well informed about world affairs and will therefore be aware of the tremendous implications of the world-wide political involvement in these matters."

I nodded, and he went on, "Bill and me are in Zermatt as the result of the kidnapping of the daughter of a leading scientist. This man is engaged in highly secret work in Geneva."

"I'm listening."

"Well, we're here to ask if you can help us with some details over our investigation into the disappearance of this girl. We believe you may know something useful as the result of your association with a certain young woman that you've been keeping company with lately."

I couldn't understand what he was getting at. These organisations would be hand in glove with the CIA, so what was his problem?

"Don't your departments keep track of each other?" I asked. "I thought you had a communications network second to none. Surely you know that Helen is free and on the way to the States with her father?"

Bill Hall stood up as he spoke to me.

"Would you enlarge on that? Can you fill us in on the details of how exactly this is taking place?"

I couldn't understand why he was acting so dumb; surely, they knew the score by now. The thought peeved me, and I spoke harshly.

"Oh hell, you don't need to waste my time with this. Let the CIA sort it out, they get paid for it, I don't."

Both men were standing now, and not liking being looked down on, I stood up as well.

Falconer was next to speak, and his voice had hardened noticeably.

"I can assure you that we are fully briefed on this affair, and Helen Linstead is still missing. Furthermore, your recent acquaintance, Miss Summers, has also disappeared."

It was the first time that Kim had been mentioned by name. I knew that she had gone to Geneva, and these two were probably expecting to find her here, and thought she'd disappeared. Could it be that she'd changed her mind about me after all?

"Well maybe she's just taken a holiday," I said. "She bloody well deserves one, after what she's just been through. The CIA will have to put another agent on her assignment if it's so pressing."

My day had suddenly brightened. It could be she was going to contact me and agree to my proposal to come to England.

My thoughts were interrupted by Bill Hall.

"Will you tell us what you know about this, and your involvement? We've checked you out and feel certain that you're not working for any government, either East or West, and we're puzzled about your role in this."

"Tell you what," I said, feeling pretty cocky now, "this business has put me to some expense, to say nothing of the inconvenience. Would your organisation be willing to reimburse me if I agree to help you?"

They looked at each other, then the young one nodded, and Falconer replied.

"I think that could be arranged. How much did you have in mind?"

"Three thousand francs — and I'd like you to confirm it with your office in Geneva now."

They each looked at each other again.

"That would be possible," Falconer said, "providing you can convince us that you've played an active part with our interests in mind." He stressed the word 'our' as he finished speaking.

I reached for the telephone. This was my lucky day. Kim was coming back to me, and the CIA or these monkey's' outfits, were going to cough up the spondulicks to finance it. I handed Falconer the phone and he got through to his office again. His conversation was rather guarded. He went on for some length, and I could hear what he was saying, but didn't know what was being said at the other end.

"It's all set," he said, putting the phone down. "If you're on the level, tell us what you know, and if it's useful to us, my office will forward you a draft for your expenses."

I told them the whole story, well almost the whole

of it, missing out the intimate parts. They interrupted now and then for me to clarify a point. Other than that, they sat in silence, and when I'd finished, they spoke in lowered voices to each other.

Falconer spoke to me.

"I believe you acted with commendable motives and considerable courage. But I'm sorry to have to tell you that all is not what it seems." He crossed to the window and stood looking out. Then he turned and continued. "In the first place the man you found in the mountain hut was not a CIA agent."

I started to protest but he stopped me.

"Let me continue. John Wallace was not with the CIA. The man you described was a known member of the DONS who we knew was operating in Italy."

"DONS?" I queried.

"The Department of National Security — the South African secret service, formally known as BOSS."

"But I saw his papers," I argued, "and it was through that I contacted Kim Summers."

"I know you believed his identity was a CIA agent, but that was just a cover he was using in case he was discovered. A genuine CIA agent wouldn't carry such identification on a mission like this outside the US."

I looked him in the eyes.

"What cover would he use? The delegation to the World Food Organisation, or perhaps the Office of Multilateral Food Distribution?" I sneered.

He didn't bat an eyelid.

"Draw your own conclusions," he said quietly.

"Well, all right then," I said. "Supposing this guy was a DONS agent, why was he carrying Kim's telephone number? She's on your team, and was working to find the professor's daughter, and get her back to her father in Geneva."

Falconer went on,

"But she didn't, and now Kim has disappeared. By what you've told us, it's now clear that she was playing a double agent's game, and that's why John Wallace had her number."

I was finding all this hard to believe, but he continued.

"By now she will have arranged for the girl to be taken to South Africa and handed over to the authorities there. That means they are now in the same position as the Russians would have been, in using the girl as a means of persuading the professor to go back there."

Was he conning me, I wondered? If what he said was true, it meant that Kim had played me for a sucker all along, and I didn't want to believe that. On the other hand, there was no apparent reason for him to invent a cock and bull story about it. Thinking back, I began to recall certain things that I'd dismissed at the time but were now beginning to make sense.

Another thought came to me.

"Well South Africa's not an Eastern Bloc country, and they lean towards the West, so if they've got the kid it can't be that bad."

I could see he didn't share my view, but he didn't comment. It was Bill Hall who took up the story.

"It all boils down to this," he said. "The professor's kid was taken by an Italian group engaged by the KGB and told to get her out of Switzerland and over to the East. Once there, the commies would use her to persuade her father to transfer his work to them, in order to be with her. We sent Kim Summers here to pick up the scent, and report back to us what she managed to find out about where the kid was being held. Unbeknown to us she was also working with the DONS.

The Italian group obviously took you to be a rival agent in the mountains, trying to discover their hideout, and took you prisoner. After you escaped, they came looking for you, and must have spotted John Wallace, who was getting close. They shot and wounded him, but he managed to get away, and that's when you found him in the hut. When you went for help you made contact with Kim, and she in turn got in touch with her DONS contact. They got her to use you in order to reach their man. You had seen the false CIA identity that he carried and assumed that both him and her were working for our side, and she was happy to play you along with the deception."

It was all beginning to make sense to me now, and I asked him to continue.

"Before the two of you got back to the hut to rescue Wallace, the Italians had found him and killed him, thinking they had put a stop to the attempt to discover

252

them. Later, when Kim phoned that night from that Italian village, she contacted the DONS, who sent that guy Renato to help her with a rescue operation. They knew it would blow her cover with us if she succeeded, but in any case, she would then have served their purpose."

It was my turn to ask some questions. I looked at Falconer.

"If all this is true, I don't understand how you came to be in Milan and followed me back here."

"That's easy," he said. "I was in Geneva believing she was working for us. I went to Milan after a tip-off that some members of an underground group were preparing to meet up with someone who had the professor's daughter."

"That would have been us," I said. "Kim, me and the kid."

"Right," he answered, "but I didn't know that at the time. When I reached Milan, my informant told me that he thought who I wanted was in the hotel. We both kept watch, and when you came out, he said you could be one of them. So, leaving him on watch, I followed you. I thought you could be going to make contact, but instead you did some shopping then returned to the hotel. Meanwhile some others had arrived and taken the kid away. I cursed my informant, who I'd left watching, for not following them, but as there was nothing more I could do, I went off to report to Geneva. When I got back you came out again, so I followed you to Milan station."

I couldn't suppress my grin, as I asked.

"When I finally shook you off at Visp, and you missed that last train up here to Zermatt, how did you manage to get here last night?"

"I got a taxi as far as Tasch, then walked here along the track. It was a God damn long way and I'm getting too old for that sort of thing."

I managed to suppress another grin, as he went on. "When I got here, I met up with Bill and he told me that he hadn't made contact with Kim, but that Kurt Van Schmid was here. We knew he was a DONS agent, so I staked out his hotel. Later that night I trailed him here, but he left soon afterwards, and I followed him to the Alpenrose. When I went in, I saw the three of you together, so I knew Kim was double crossing us, and Van Schmid had probably gone there to warn her to clear out."

This was making sense now, but it wasn't pleasing me.

"What happened after Kim and me left?"

"Van Schmid and me got mixed up in a fight that broke out, and he gave me the slip and got away. When I got out, you two had gone. I knew that Van Schmid had come to this hotel earlier, so I came here, but the desk clerk told me that you'd both checked out. I knew you couldn't leave Zermatt last night, but there were too many other hotels to check at that time of night, so I went back to Bill's hotel for the night."

254

"That's about it then," I said. "There's nothing I can add to that."

It was Bill Hall's turn to speak.

"Kim is still one jump ahead of us. I checked the station, but she wasn't there, and later I found out that she'd flown out with that private chopper service."

I looked at him as I spoke.

"She's top of the class for resourcefulness."

"Is there any more you can tell us?" Falconer asked me.

"Well, she left me sometime last night or early this morning — I can't be more specific because I crashed out and didn't wake till late."

"We must prevent her from getting his daughter to South Africa; the consequences of that will be too damaging for us," he said.

"You mean it will give them the same sort of political bargaining weapon that Agripower provides you with," I challenged.

I saw immediately that my comment had not gone down well with either of them.

"So, when do I get my expenses?" I asked.

They both walked to the door, preparing to leave. Bill Hall opened it for Falconer to go through. Falconer paused and turned to look at me.

"Let me put it this way, Mr Sands, if you don't have enough cash to pay the hotel bill, I hear they're always in need of a good janitor."

He turned and walked away with Bill Hall close

behind.

"Thanks' for nothing," I called after them. "Have the coffee on me."

I closed the door of my room and sat down on the bed. So, Kim had skipped, and the DONS had the kid, and I couldn't help admiring the way she had pulled it off. I still found it hard to believe that our brief affair had meant nothing to her. Perhaps it was because it hurt my pride — or vanity.

What was that old saying I'd thought of earlier? 'Ships that pass in the night'.

One thing was sure, she'd left me, but I couldn't accept that she'd just strung me along and felt nothing. I was sure that I'd almost convinced her to come away with me, but her mission had prevented it.

As I packed to leave, I wondered how much of what she had told me about herself was true. Did what she'd said about her husband's death, and her subsequent recruitment, really happen like that? Now I would probably never know.

Collecting my gear, I took a final look around, and went down to settle my bill. Leaving the hotel, I wondered if it was worth going to Riederalp for a couple of days or staying in Brig and trying to convince Titsalina that I didn't suffer with amnesia.

Outside, the clear morning air filled my lungs and revitalised my enthusiasm. Why not have a couple of hours skiing here, then go to Brig?

Why not?

I hired some skis and decided on the Sunnegga-Blauherd run, as it was the best for the time I had.

I skied until lunch, then enjoyed several more runs in excellent conditions. Calling it a day, I caught the train to Brig and arrived in time to visit my bank. I would check my account, and then after a night at the Eggishorn, I'd collect my car and return home.

Arriving at the bank, Herr Eyer saw me and came to the counter. Greeting me by name, he shook my hand, and he smiled as he spoke. "I was hoping you would visit the bank today, Mr Sands, we have a message for you from Geneva."

"Geneva?" I queried.

"Yes, that's right. It was telephoned to us not long ago. One moment, I will fetch it for you."

He hurried away and I stood wondering what it might be.

Returning to the counter, he handed me a folded sheet of paper.

I unfolded it and read, 'Darling, H now safely en route to Johannesburg. My destination Paris. Hope that you're still in the pink. Sorry I had to leave. K.'

I read it again as Herr Eyer waited. So, she'd seen Helen off to South Africa, and it confirmed what Falconer had told me. But why would she bother to let me know, unless she was not wanting things to end here?

"Was there an address or phone number?" I asked Herr Eyer.

"No, just that message. Can I do anything else for

you?"

"Yes, I'd like some French francs, I think I'll spend a few days in Paris on my way home."

Leaving the bank, I passed a bookshop, and something I glimpsed in the doorway stopped me dead in my tracks.

"Christ!" I exclaimed. "I'm in dead trouble."

I'd noticed a metal stand, displaying coloured postcards, and I realised that I hadn't sent anything home since I arrived. Selecting one with a skier making a descent by parachute, I took it inside and paid for it together with a pen and stamp.

After addressing it, I wrote:

'Dear Flo,

Having a good time. Skiing great. Weather a bit mixed. See you soon.

Matt.'

I went outside, slipped it through the flap in the yellow post box on the wall, and strode off down the road to collect my car.

END